"We'd Better Get Something Straight.

"I have no intention of looking over my shoulder every time the two of us are alone together."

"Aw, Gussie," Cash teased. "Is that any way to talk to the man of your dreams?"

"Man of my dreams! I don't even like you! No one invited you here, and if you left tomorrow, no one would miss you."

Cash grinned. "You would."

"Like hell I would!" Gus screeched. Her nerves were all but shattered, and this idiot man just kept grinning at her. "You think you're just too cute for words, don't you? Well, you're wrong. You irritate me every minute we're together."

"What you call irritation, honey, I call chemistry."

Dear Reader,

We here at Silhouette Desire just couldn't resist bringing you another special theme month. Have you ever wondered what it is about our heroes that enables them to win the heroines' love? Of course, these men have undeniable sex appeal, and they have charm (loads of it!), and even if they're rough around the edges, you know that, deep down, they have tender hearts.

In a way, their magnetism, their charisma, is simply indescribable. These men are . . . simply Irresistible! This month, we think we've picked six heroes who are going to knock your socks off! And when these six irresistible men meet six *very* unattainable women, passion flares, sparks fly—and *you* get hours of reading pleasure!

And what month would be complete without a terrific *Man of the Month?* Delightful Dixie Browning has created a man to remember in Stone McCloud, the hero of *Lucy and the Stone. Man of the Month* fun just keeps on coming in upcoming months, with exciting love stories by Jackie Merritt, Joan Hohl, Barbara Boswell, Annette Broadrick, Lass Small and a *second* 1994 *Man of the Month* book by Ann Major.

So don't miss a single Silhouette Desire book! And, until next month, happy reading from . . .

Lucia Macro
Senior Editor

Please address questions and book requests to:
Reader Service
U.S.: P.O. Box 1325, Buffalo, NY 14269
Canadian: P.O. Box 1050, Niagara Falls, Ont. L2E 7G7

JACKIE MERRITT

PERSISTENT LADY

SILHOUETTE *Desire*®
Published by Silhouette Books
America's Publisher of Contemporary Romance

SILHOUETTE BOOKS

ISBN 0-373-05854-3

PERSISTENT LADY

JACKIE MERRITT

and her husband live just outside of Las Vegas, Nevada. An accountant for many years, Jackie has happily traded numbers for words. Next to family, books are her greatest joy. She started writing in 1987, and her efforts paid off in 1988 with the publication of her first novel. When she's not writing or enjoying a good book, Jackie dabbles in watercolor painting and has been known to tickle the ivories in her spare time.

Prologue

This was it, the farewell get-together for the three Saxon brothers. They had met in a quiet cocktail lounge and ordered drinks, and now were attempting normalcy without much success. Each felt the drama of the evening and wondered in his own mind if he wasn't overly exaggerating an ordinary event. After all, they weren't heading for the ends of the earth. Montana, Nevada and Oregon weren't all that far apart, and besides, they hadn't lived on top of one another since high school.

Yet Cash, Rush and Chance Saxon found joking difficult tonight, though they tried. "Have you heard the one about...?" preceded stories that merited a hearty laugh and instead fell a little flat.

It was just that the past several weeks had caused such an upheaval in their lives. Everything familiar had vanished almost overnight. Their beloved grandfather had died, and that sorrow had barely been faced when the brothers were told by Robert Teale, the family's attorney, not to expect anything much from Gerald Saxon's estate. In short, the

money was gone, the house, the cars, the yacht, the polo
ponies, everything the brothers had grown up with.

It was a blow none of them had seen coming. They were
nearly penniless and the initial shock had been staggering.
To their credit, they weren't sitting around mourning their
enormous losses, though the death of their grandfather
would be felt for a long time to come. Instead they had decided to salvage what they could from the estate and get on
with their lives. There were three financially weak businesses remaining. After discussing their choices, Chance, the
eldest, was going to Montana to do what he could with the
cattle ranch, Rush's destination was Nevada and a house
construction company and Cash, the middle brother, was
heading for Oregon and a logging operation. Their departures were drawing nigh. Tonight they were saying goodbye.

They were well-dressed, handsome men with a strong
family resemblance. Each was tall and lean with abundant
dark hair and electric-blue eyes. They were educated and
intelligent, and they had all three spent their thirty-odd years
in mostly pleasurable pastimes. That was over. It was time
to stand up and be counted.

The conversation turned to the personal possessions they
had each sold to raise money. Keepsakes had been stored.
Their packing was nearing completion. There had been a
hundred other departures in their lives, but none like this.

"I've been thinking," Cash said quietly. "We were
damned lucky that Granddad took us in when Mother and
Dad died in that plane crash."

"Agreed," Chance replied. "I was five, which made you
three, Cash. Rush was only a year old. Yes, we were fortunate that Granddad cared about us."

"He was made of strong stuff," Rush put in. "Yet he
never said no to any of us, did he?"

"He loved us," Cash said. "I'm not sure I realized that
until recently. He was always there, yet I can't remember
him ever mentioning love." His eyes rested on his brothers'
faces. "Can you?"

Rush gave his head a shake. "I can't."

Chance took a swallow from his glass and set it down. "Maybe we inherited that reticent gene from Granddad. Have either of you ever told someone you love them? I know I haven't."

"Not even a woman?" Cash questioned.

The brothers exchanged man-to-man grins. "Well...not when I meant it," Chance admitted. "I suppose saying it and meaning it are two different things. You know, it's kind of odd that none of us are married."

"We've got plenty of time," Rush said. "I know I'm in no hurry."

"Obviously none of us are," Chance returned dryly. "These past few weeks have made me stop and think, too, Cash, about a lot of things."

"About marriage?" Rush asked with obvious surprise.

"Not specifically, but it's certainly a part of life, little brother. Family's what's important, Rush." Chance included both brothers in his serious gaze. "We weren't only lucky to have Granddad, we're lucky to have each other."

"That we are," Cash soberly agreed. "We've got to stay in touch."

"We can call each other," Rush said.

Chance nodded. They had been speaking with emotion. Their bond was strong and sure, going even beyond their blood ties to genuine affection. To love.

He cleared his throat. The words wouldn't come. But maybe that was all right. The three of them knew how they all felt.

When they said goodbye an hour later, they hugged and pounded each other's backs.

"Christmas," Cash said suddenly. Chance and Rush gave him a quizzical look. "Come hell or high water, let's get together for Christmas."

December was six months away, but Cash's suggestion settled into each man's system in a comforting way. "Get together where?" Rush questioned.

"We can decide that later," Chance said. "But I like taking that idea with me. Christmas it is."

They shook hands on the pact. Whatever obstacles they encountered in Nevada, Montana and Oregon, whatever problems, failures or successes, they would see each other in December.

They walked away from each other with lighter hearts, all because of a simple plan to meet at Christmas.

One

Cash Saxon was admittedly anxious to get to his destination in Oregon. He wasn't a hundred percent sold on his two brothers' eagerness for the unknown future they all faced, but his own had seemingly grown to unignorable proportions.

During the trip west, Cash had asked himself why. Why had a life-style he knew nothing about suddenly become so tantalizing? Was it the challenge? The macho image of loggers he remembered seeing in magazine layouts depicting the Northwest's timber industry? Maybe it was the independence of standing on his own two feet for the first time in his life, or simply because he liked jeans and boots and loved the outdoors.

Cash was armed with as much information as Robert Teale, the attorney, had possessed. Cash knew there was a partner involved in the logging operation, an arrangement neither Chance nor Rush would have to deal with in their respective businesses. But having a partner didn't alarm Cash, quite the contrary. James Parrish—Big Jim, Teale had called him—had been running the company for a long time, and Cash looked at the association as beneficial. After all, what did he know about logging? Oh, he had a passive knowledge from books, television and magazine articles. But he had no practical experience, a condition he planned to rectify as quickly as possible. He would work alongside of Big Jim and learn the business from the ground up.

Driving along on a winding mountain road, Cash chuckled at his analogy. Learning the logging business "from the ground up" was probably the only way to do it.

To locate the Saxon-Parrish logging camp, Cash had been following the instructions given to him by Teale. The camp was deep into the Cascade Range of mountains, on high ground. Though the day was rapidly evolving into evening, the temperature was still warm enough to drive with the windows down. The moist, aromatic scent of the rich forest made Cash feel alive. The setting sun filtered through the tall Douglas firs to dapple the road ahead of Cash's Wagoneer, a used vehicle he had purchased in Portland after flying in from the East. Each curve in the road revealed more forest and another scenic setting. Cash's excitement mounted as the detailed directions indicated he was getting very close to the camp.

Around a final curve he spotted buildings through the trees. His smile broadened, and he drove into a clearing surrounded by forest and various structures. Cash stopped the Wagoneer to take a look. To the left was a shop with a large diesel truck inside. Straight ahead was a building that could be anything; Cash thought maybe it was a place for the men to sleep. Another structure looked like it could be a place for the men to eat. To the right was a log building, maybe an office. Deeper into the trees was a log cabin…Big Jim's quarters?

Most of Cash's conclusions were guesswork. There were a few men in sight, one inside the shop who he could see was working on the truck, and several idling near the building he thought was the bunkhouse.

He switched off the ignition and got out of the Wagoneer. That's when he saw the sign: Parrish-Saxon Logging

Company. He frowned, because Robert Teale had referred to the operation as Saxon-Parrish.

Deciding that he wasn't going to let second billing bother him, he headed toward the men near the bunkhouse.

"Evening," he called.

The three men eyed him curiously. "Evening."

Cash walked up to them. "Are you Saxon-Parrish men?"

"Parrish-Saxon, don't you mean?" one of them said.

"Whatever," Cash said with a faint grin. "At least I'm in the right place." He jerked his thumb toward the log cabin in the trees. "Is that the Parrish home?"

All three men nodded. One of them said, "Sure is. You here to see Gus?"

"Gus?" Cash was suddenly uncertain. Teale had talked about James Parrish—Big Jim, not Gus. But maybe Gus was another nickname. "Will I find Gus at the cabin?"

"Should be there," the more talkative fellow agreed.

Cash grinned, again faintly. "Thanks. I'll go on over." He could feel the men's eyes on his back as he walked. He could have introduced himself, but thought Big Jim—or Gus, if that was how he was known in this camp—might appreciate meeting him first.

The clearing gave way to a path through the trees, which ended at a set of three steps leading to the front porch of the cabin. The building was larger than he'd initially thought, Cash realized as he climbed the stairs and crossed the porch to the door. He rapped and then let his gaze wander while he waited for Gus.

The place was beautiful. Rustic, even a little crude, but beautiful. The tall trees were as imposing as a cathedral, shading the clearing, towering over the buildings. He could feel the encroachment of nighttime's lower temperature at this high elevation. It was energizing. Excitement raced in his blood. This fantastic place was his. His and Big Jim's, that is.

The door opened. "Yes?"

Cash brought his eyes around to a very small woman with red hair and a striking face. Her attractive, slightly turned-up nose was sprinkled with freckles, and her determined little chin bore a hint of a cleft below a startlingly pretty mouth.

He kept looking. She was dressed in snug faded jeans and a blue T-shirt. Her figure was...

Cash's mouth became strangely dry. This little woman's figure was maybe the best he'd ever seen. Full breasts, rounded hips and thighs, and a tiny waist if the indentation of that T-shirt was at all accurate.

"Yes?" she repeated with a raised eyebrow.

Cash felt warmth in his neck and face. He'd been caught staring, and all he could do was pretend not to notice that arched, disapproving eyebrow.

"I'm Cash Saxon." He saw the eyebrow drop.

"Did you say *Saxon?*"

Clearly he'd surprised her. "Saxon, yes. Cash Saxon."

"Um...I'm...Gus Parrish."

"You're Gus?" Cash couldn't help a short laugh. "I'm sorry, but you don't look like any Gus I've ever met before." The comment was intended to be complimentary.

"Do I look more like an *Augusta* to you?" Gus asked with some coolness.

"Actually...no." Cash laughed again. "Sorry." He wondered why he kept wanting to laugh. Something about this easy-to-look-at little woman made him feel good, just as this whole setup did. The area. The mountains and dense forest. His role here. He felt an affinity with it all, including Gus, who was a woman he undoubtedly would have noticed in any setting.

Gus wasn't nearly as tickled. "Believe me," she said dryly, "I've heard it all before. Would you like to come in?" A Saxon showing up on her doorstep after all this time was a little tough to figure. But he had a right to be here, however belated his arrival.

"Yes, thanks." Gus wasn't Big Jim, that much was certain. A daughter, maybe. Cash's urge to laugh died rather abruptly as the word *wife* popped into his mind.

Gus stepped back and held the door open. While her unexpected and startling visitor entered, she gave him a quick once-over. Like her, he was wearing jeans. Unlike her, his were pressed and creased and not bought at a discount store. His boots—of the cowboy variety—were as shiny as a mirror, also expensive, she figured. For that matter, the man himself looked expensive, crisp and sure of himself and a little too good-looking to evoke immediate trust.

The door opened onto a large room that Cash decided was the cabin's living room. One wall was solid rock and contained a huge fireplace. There was a sofa, and a multitude of comfortable-looking chairs, tables, lamps and bright rag rugs on the gleaming wood floor. It was a warm, inviting room, and seemed perfectly suited to the area.

Gus gestured with a wide sweep of her hand. "Sit down."

"Thank you." His gaze moved around the room as he sank onto a chair. "This cabin is great."

"It's a log house, not a cabin, but thanks." Gus chose a chair that faced Saxon's. His arrival was sinking in and questions were beginning to form. Her first stab at conversation was a bluntly stated, "This is a surprise."

Cash looked at her. "I suppose it is. Are you related to James Parrish?"

"His daughter. What can I do for you, Mr. Saxon?"

Big Jim's daughter. Cash felt himself relaxing and feeling more at home. "I appreciate your courtesy, but I probably should be talking to him."

Gus stiffened. "Dad died four months ago. Didn't you know?"

For a few seconds the life drained out of Cash, replaced by a flood tide of embarrassment. How could he not know? Maybe because he hadn't known *anything* about the logging company until a few weeks ago. Maybe because he'd read the papers Teale had given him without digesting crucial facts. Maybe because there'd been no mention of James Parrish's death in that information.

The shock began fading. "I'm sorry, Gus. You'd have to know my background to understand, and I'm not using it as an excuse. Coming here so uninformed is unforgivable, but all I can do is apologize."

She studied Saxon. He was red-faced and it hadn't been her intention to heap guilt on the man. Looking away from him, she murmured, "It's all right. Let's talk about something else." She brought slightly harder eyes back to her visitor. "Let's discuss why you felt a need to talk to Dad at all. To my knowledge, this company has operated without a Saxon on the premises since its inception fourteen years ago."

"How did it get started?" Cash questioned, truly interested. "How did your father and my grandfather meet to form their partnership?"

Gus frowned. "Why...I don't think I know. Does it matter?"

"Guess not. Granddad had his financial fingers in a lot of different pots, and I was just curious. He's gone, too. Less than a month ago."

"You have my sympathy." Perhaps because of their grievous common ground, Gus became friendlier. "Would you like a cup of coffee?"

Cash's empty stomach was growling. He'd driven for hours to reach this place and hadn't had dinner. "Yes, thanks."

Gus got to her feet. "Cream or sugar?"

"Black, please."

Cash did a little worrying during Gus's absence. The company was still in operation, apparently, but without Big Jim, indicating that someone else was managing it. That was the person he needed to see, he decided just as Gus returned with two mugs.

She set one on the table next to Cash's chair, then resumed her previous seat. She'd done some worrying in the kitchen, too, considering Cash Saxon's appearance from several different angles and discovering she wasn't very thrilled with any of them.

Cash took a swallow and found the coffee to his liking, strong and hot. "Who's running the company, Gus?"

"I am."

"You?"

The surprised look on his face was almost funny. She understood that he hadn't fully grasped what he'd heard when he said, "You mean you're running the office."

"I *mean* I'm running the *company*," Gus stated flatly. "The office, the woods, the men, the partnership. Do you have a problem with that?"

Damned right he had a problem with that. Cash took a drink of coffee while narrowing his eyes at Gus Parrish over the rim. She worked in the woods? No bigger than a peanut, and she told those burly men out there what to do? The ones he'd seen looked like tough loggers, men with muscles and weathered faces. Gus looked like a soft little kitten in spite of that head of fiery hair—the kind of woman a man would like to cuddle on his lap, and then pick up and carry to... his bed.

Cash cleared his throat. "This is really tough to take in, Gus. I mean, I came here expecting..."

When his voice trailed off, Gus picked up the thread. "Expecting what, Mr. Saxon?"

"Call me Cash." He set the mug down on the table. "I *didn't* expect a female partner."

"No, you expected to meet Big Jim Parrish, and instead you have to deal with me. I'm the Parrish in the Parrish-Saxon arrangement now, but are you the Saxon?"

Their gazes tangled across the space between their chairs. Cash swallowed. Gus stared. Finally he said, "I'm him."

Gus told herself not to be alarmed. There hadn't been a Saxon on this mountain for fourteen years that she knew of, and this guy was a city slicker if she'd ever seen one. He wasn't apt to hang around this unpretentious, isolated camp for long. Probably just got the idea to check on a pile of inherited assets after his grandfather's death.

"Well, I'm sure it won't be a problem," she said calmly, belying the overfast beat of her heart. Somehow she knew Cash was going to be a problem. Way back in her mind was conviction and dread. And there was something else that bothered her: his good looks. Not that she didn't appreciate striking masculinity, but this wasn't the guy to get silly about when she'd deliberately avoided attractive men since her divorce. Two years had passed, but she still wasn't ready for another dose of the male ego.

The house was getting dark. Noticing, Gus got up and switched on several lamps. She remained standing. "Are you planning to spend the night? If so, you can stay in the bunkhouse with the men. There are a couple of extra beds."

Cash rose slowly. "You don't understand. I'm not just here for the night."

Gus's stomach dropped clear to her knees. She only managed to maintain what she hoped was a detached expression through supreme effort. "You're not? How long are you planning to stay?"

There was no easy way to put this, Cash decided. Obviously Gus Parrish hoped his visit was of short duration, and she might as well hear the unvarnished truth right now. "I'm here to stay."

"To stay?" she echoed numbly.

"Permanently," Cash supplied.

A silence thick enough to slice was suddenly between them. Gus tried to think, to grasp what was happening, and all she could do was mourn the loss of her position here. Not that she would take any sass from a greenhorn partner. When her father became ill and disabled nearly two years ago, she had come home and taken over, and because of Big Jim's tutelage, she was as good in the woods as he'd been. It was ironic that he hadn't let her work in the business while growing up when she'd begged and pleaded for that very goal, and then had leaned so heavily on her after he could no longer handle it himself.

Regardless, this was her life now, and she loved it. Not once had she worried about one of those faceless, barely acknowledged Saxons suddenly showing up and demanding recognition. Ordinarily Augusta Parrish didn't panic. Her small stature was deceiving, and anyone who equated her lack of height to a lack of strength was badly mistaken. She might be tiny and she might look soft and defenseless, but she was a strong, levelheaded, usually even-tempered woman. This evening, however, she felt panicked and angry and emotionally distraught, and the one person to blame was standing right in front of her.

Her lips thinned to a grim line. "Are you telling me that you intend to intrude on the Parrish-Saxon partnership after all this time?"

Gus's choice of words struck Cash as overbearing and judgmental. His own mouth thinned. "No, I'm telling you that I intend to claim my fifty percent of the *Saxon*-Parrish partnership."

Gus's eyes widened. "Why, after all these years, is this simple little operation so interesting to a high and mighty Saxon?" she asked with her gray-green eyes flashing.

Cash turned his head to conceal his rising anger. He hadn't come here to fight with anyone, certainly not a pint-size woman he hadn't even known existed until a few minutes ago.

He returned cooler eyes to Gus. "I think it would be best if we both made the best of things, don't you? To be perfectly honest, I'm no more thrilled with you as a partner than you are with me, but sniping at each other isn't going to help the situation, *nor,* I might point out, change it. I'm here, and I'm staying here."

"Not in this house, you're not!"

"It never occurred to me to stay in this house! I'll build my own damned house! In the meantime I'll stay in the bunkhouse!"

Gus turned her back, shoved her hands into the back pockets of her jeans and paced a circle around the room. She was steaming and couldn't seem to control the boiling of her blood. Cash was here to stay. She'd like nothing better than to kick his arrogant butt clean off the mountain, but everything was half his—the whole damned mountain, the equipment, the buildings, this *house!*

Cash watched her pacing. His anger began to fade. She was the sweetest-looking little woman he'd ever seen—shapely, pretty and sexy. Her feet were clad in moccasins; she was at least a foot shorter than he was, and perfectly proportioned from her short but luxuriant, flaming red hair to those miniature moccasins. He'd rather kiss her than fight with her, he thought, surprising himself by the erotic nature of his swinging mood.

"Look," he said sensibly. "Let's both sleep on it. My coming here was a shock. Even your father would have been surprised."

"To say the least," Gus drawled dryly. She wasn't all that thrilled with the animosity brewing, either. Maybe there was a way to disenchant Cash Saxon and get rid of him, but a screaming session wasn't it. He had gotten angry as quickly as she had, so he wasn't going to be bullied off the mountain.

"You don't have to stay in the bunkhouse," she said tonelessly. "There's an apartment in the office building. It's not fancy, but you'll have some privacy."

Her unexpected generosity surprised Cash. "Thanks. I appreciate privacy."

Gus gritted her teeth. "Come along and I'll show you the way."

Darkness had fallen in earnest. Gus lit the path with a flashlight. There were lights in the bunkhouse, Cash saw, though the building he'd thought might be the cookhouse and dining room was dark. "Any chance of getting some dinner?" he asked while trailing Gus's footsteps.

She stopped. "You haven't had dinner?" She sighed heavily, a put-upon, long-suffering sigh that grated on Cash's nerves.

"No, I haven't," he admitted dourly.

Without another word on that matter, Gus veered toward the cookshack. "Watch for rocks and stumps," she yelled over her shoulder. "It's easy to trip over something in the dark."

"No kidding," Cash muttered under his breath as the toe of his boot caught on something and he nearly went sprawling.

Gus opened the door of the cookshack and hit the wall switch just inside for the ceiling lights. "Come on in. There's usually something in the kitchen for a sandwich."

Noting the plastic-covered tables in the first room, Cash followed Gus to the kitchen. It had an immense gas range, long counters and worktables, and huge pots and pans stacked on shelves. Gus pulled open the door of an enor-

►

mous refrigerator and peered in. "There's roast beef. Will that do?"

"Anything is fine."

Gus laid out bread, the plate of roast beef and several jars of condiments on a table. "Help yourself."

Realizing that Augusta Parrish had no intention of treating him as a guest made Cash smile, though he kept the reaction to himself and got busy making his sandwich. The bread was sliced thick and smelled wonderful, homemade, he figured, and the beef was lean and from a good cut. Obviously the partnership didn't stint on food for its men, which met with Cash's approval.

Looking at Gus, he raised the sandwich for a big bite. "Do you do the cooking?"

Her features tensed. "I told you what I do."

He couldn't resist goading her. She needed goading worse than any woman he'd ever met. She didn't like him being here and was probably planning to make his life as miserable as she could manage. It wasn't a pleasant prospect, and he wasn't going to sit on his hands and make it easy for her.

"True," he drawled. "But with you being a woman and all, I thought maybe—"

"A woman and *all?* What do you mean by 'all'?"

Cash looked her up and down. "Well, you sure don't have the usual build for a logger."

Gus's face flamed. "I will not tolerate that sort of innuendo from you or any other man! What do you know about it anyway? I'd be willing to bet this is the first logging camp you've ever set foot in."

Nonchalantly Cash nodded. "You'd win the bet. But how many women loggers do *you* know? Especially women who are only knee-high to a grasshopper and filling out jeans and a T-shirt the way you do?"

She wanted to smack him one, a healthy pop right on his nasty mouth. There'd been a few men on the job who'd said things like that to her, worse, in fact, and she'd set them straight real fast.

But she hadn't blushed and gotten too warm in the process. She hadn't felt the heat of their gazes inside her, as she was doing now. Her involuntary response infuriated her.

"You think you're pretty hot stuff, don't you?" she said derisively. "You're nothing here, Saxon, and I'm going to enjoy every mistake you make."

Her anger was out in the open again, which was where Cash preferred it. They may as well understand each other right from the get-go. "What I am is your partner, Gussie Parrish, and don't you forget it."

She drew herself up to her full height, all five feet one inches of it. She loathed that name, but she suspected Saxon would use it constantly if she let him know. She picked up the flashlight. "If you want me to show you the apartment, take your sandwich and come right now. I'm not going to dawdle around this kitchen half the night."

Grinning, Cash followed her out.

The apartment was a barely furnished bedroom and a bath with a tin shower, but it looked great to Cash. The bed was clean, he saw from a quick inspection after Gus had stormed out. He carried in his suitcases, hung up a few things in the minuscule closet and took a shower. The pipes creaked and groaned, but there was adequate hot water.

After switching off the lights, Cash crawled into bed with a satisfied grunt. He had opened a window, and a cool, bordering on chilly, breeze drifted across the bed. He hiked up the blankets and closed his eyes, ready for sleep.

But instead of relaxing, he felt tension. In his mind was an image of Augusta Parrish. And his thoughts became sexual in nature.

Unnerved, he turned to his side and stared at the window. He could feel the breeze and smell the forest. This was his home now.

But why in hell was he thinking about sex and Gus in the same breath? She certainly wasn't going to do some kind of about-face and suddenly like him. He had disrupted her life, challenged her authority and told her to get used to it, all in the space of a few minutes.

No, she wasn't going to suddenly like him, and even if they managed to attain a sensible working relationship, she would never allow any more than that.

"Forget she's a woman," he mumbled to himself.

It was good advice, and the thought he held on to until sleep took him.

Gus wasn't as fortunate. She rolled and tossed for hours. The situation was impossible and she hated it. Saxon's infiltration was going to bring her nothing but trouble. Her life had been orderly, not particularly easy, but orderly. The logging business was a tough row to hoe, and she didn't need the additional burden of a greenhorn city slicker tripping over his own feet or hers every time she turned around.

Yet there was no other job she wanted to do. Coming home, even to tend her ill father and help out with the business, had felt like a release from oppression. She'd been living in the heart of Los Angeles, working at a job she hadn't liked, and returning to Oregon's cool green mountains had lifted her flagging spirits as nothing else could have.

For a while there'd been hope for her father's recovery, but then a second and a third heart attack had made them all—Big Jim, several doctors and herself—face the painful truth. By then Gus had been running the Parrish-Saxon Company, and during one of their final conversations Big Jim had bluntly told her to stay put after he was gone and keep on doing the same good job she'd been doing.

Later Gus had wept, but at the time she'd swallowed her tears and vowed to follow his advice, for him as much as for herself. And no damned Saxon was going to step in at this late date and take over, not as long as there was breath in her body.

For the briefest of moments Gus let Saxon's handsome face and lean body replace her bitter thoughts. But at a discomfiting jolt of physical awareness, she quickly reached for bitterness again and concentrated on tomorrow.

Somehow she had to convince Saxon that he was in the wrong place at the wrong time. If she didn't succeed, she was in for one hell of an unsettling future.

She *had* to succeed. What other choice did she have?

TWO

Cash was awakened by the sound of voices outside in the compound. From the dim light in the room, the hour had to be before full dawn. He felt yesterday's excitement welling again; this was his first real day in the logging business.

But Cash's thoughts immediately jumped to Gus Parrish. Last night's unfriendly and threatening sparring match had been foolish and unnecessary. He'd deliberately baited her about her size and gender. It was an unusual deviation from Cash's normal response to an attractive woman, and he had to wonder about it. Gus set off strange reactions—that urge to laugh over her name, for one. Her name wasn't funny—inappropriate, maybe, but not funny.

He had to try harder with Gus. Getting along only made sense. This wasn't a game. Cash needed to learn, and Gus, apparently, was the best person to teach him. A laugh rippled out of Cash, despite his decision to take Gus seriously. Learning the logging business from a half-pint woman had a comical feel, and he couldn't seem to get past the humor in it.

He got out of bed eager to begin. After shaving and dressing, Cash left the apartment and headed toward the cookhouse. He stopped to look around. The clearing was silent and vacant. Where was everyone?

Frowning, he continued on to the cookhouse and went inside. There were sounds coming from the kitchen, but the dining room was empty. He approached the kitchen doorway and saw a heavy-set woman about fifty years old kneading dough on one of the long tables. A white apron covered the front of her blue cotton dress, and her graying brown hair was tidily confined in a net.

She looked up. "Good morning."

Cash offered a smile. "Hello. Did I miss breakfast?"

"Afraid you did. Everyone's already gone to work." The woman went back to her dough. Her fleshy arms bounced as she worked. Cash was fascinated with her manipulation of the large mass of dough on the table. "If you're hungry, there's coffee and sweet rolls on that counter over there."

"Thanks." Cash poured himself a mug of coffee and helped himself to a roll. "I'm Cash Saxon."

"Gus told me to expect you," the woman replied. "Name's Mandy Willis. Have a seat, if you want."

There were two chairs in the kitchen, and Cash moved one of them next to the counter and sat down. "Is that bread you're making?"

"Sure is."

"I sampled some of your bread last night. Best I've ever eaten."

"Bread's not hard to make. Can't figure out why young gals today don't take the time. That's all it boils down to, a little time and effort. Always make my own bread. Crew appreciates it."

Cash smiled. "I'm sure they do. Been working here long, Mandy?"

"Four, five years, I guess. It's a good job. My quarters are through that door there." She nodded at a door nestled between the refrigerator and a cabinet, and then turned the dough over to knead it from another direction. Her gaze rose to Cash. "How's that coffee? It's been made awhile."

"It's fine, thanks." Cash reached for another roll. "These cinnamon rolls are fantastic."

"Yes, they're good," Mandy agreed. "Where do you hail from, Cash?"

"East Coast. New York."

"One coast to the other, hmm? Do you like it out here, or haven't you been here long enough to know?"

"I like it. I've spent time in Oregon before. Not in these mountains, but I can't imagine anyone not finding this place beautiful."

"Oh, it's easy on the eye, no doubt about that."

Gus came in. "Oh, there you are."

Cash got to his feet while his gaze washed over Gus. She was wearing jeans, a plaid cotton shirt, heavy boots and a hard hat, and he felt the urge to laugh again. Fortunately he was able to stifle the impulse. "Good morning. I thought you'd gone with everyone else."

"I've been to the logging site and back again," she said briskly. She hadn't lingered in the woods this morning. Once the men were working and she'd seen that things were going smoothly, she'd jumped into her pickup and headed back. The logging job wasn't a problem today; Cash Saxon was. The sooner she managed to get rid of him, the happier she'd be, which couldn't be accomplished from the other side of the mountain.

She poured herself a mug of coffee and regarded Cash while she drank it. He looked rested and handsome and his damned jeans were creased.

"Thought you might like a tour this morning," she said coolly.

"Yes, I would. Mandy, thanks for the coffee and rolls."

Gus led Cash outside, using the kitchen's back door. "I'll show you around the compound, then drive you to the current job site."

"Fine," Cash said agreeably. Gus seemed inclined toward a truce this morning, and he certainly wasn't going to provoke her.

They walked to the next building, and Cash peered into the bunkhouse. They toured the shop, where she introduced Cash to the mechanic working on the diesel truck, and said when they were outside again, "There's always at least one truck broken down. All of the company equipment is old and maintenance is costly."

They headed for the office. Inside were two scarred desks and a variety of mismatched file cabinets. An ancient typewriter sat on a stand, and the calculators on the desks were large, clumsy-looking and badly outdated. Gus watched Cash taking it all in. Guilt hit her hard enough to steal her breath, and she sucked in air, turning her back so he wouldn't notice.

"Well," he finally said, not knowing what else to say. He was disappointed with the office equipment and trying not to show it. There should be a computer, or at least an up-to-date typewriter and modern calculators, he thought. He glanced at Gus. "Who does the book work?"

"I keep up the payroll, the checkbook and the daily production records. Once a month I bring everything to a C.P.A. in Hamilton. He puts out the financial statements."

Cash frowned at the calculators. "How do you manage on those things?"

"They work," Gus said noncommittally. She couldn't say more. Deceit wasn't easy for her, especially planned deceit. Very early this morning she had exchanged the much better quality typewriter and calculators for these old relics, which had been packed away in the storage room in her house.

Still, it was only a very small deceit, she told herself. The company certainly couldn't be labeled affluent, and all she'd done was exaggerate the truth a little.

"There isn't any extra money for fancy equipment," she said with a sidelong glance at Cash.

"I wasn't hoping for fancy," Cash dryly replied. Thoughtfully he rubbed his mouth. "Well, I'm ready to see the job site if you are."

"Come along then." Again Gus led the way, this time to her pickup parked nearby. She slid behind the wheel while Cash climbed in through the passenger door. "If you want a full breakfast," she announced, "you'll have to get up at four-thirty with everyone else. Mandy puts breakfast out at five o'clock in the morning."

"I'll be up tomorrow morning," Cash returned evenly. "Tell me about the logging site."

"Certainly. This entire mountain belongs to the partnership. We log selectively, which means we only harvest timber of a mature age and size. The actual logging site is moved about every two weeks. My father laid out the plan and method years ago, and by adhering to it, we will never run out of timber. As long as there's a demand for logs to turn into lumber and other wood products, this company will stay in business."

She'd spoken proudly, Cash noted, and maybe she should. He'd read about selective tree harvesting, and it made good sense for a long-term operation. But longevity wasn't the only consideration in a successful business.

"From the financial statements, the company doesn't net a whole lot of profit," he said, turning his head to look at her. "Would you say that's because of production rates, or other factors?"

Gus took her eyes from the road to send him a sharp glance. "There's nothing wrong with our production rates."

"Then it must be other factors. You mentioned the high cost of equipment maintenance."

"The alternative to keeping what we have operational is enormous replacement debt," Gus said pointedly. "If you've studied the statements, you have to know we don't go into debt for fancy equipment."

There was that word again, *fancy*. Everything the company didn't possess apparently came under the heading of "fancy" for Gus, which didn't compute for Cash. If exorbitant repair and maintenance costs were eating up profits, why not change procedure and buy equipment that wasn't constantly in the shop?

But Cash felt too new to the mountain to be making any innovative suggestions. And Lord knew he didn't have any business background to back up his opinion, even if his idea seemed like the simplest concept.

The morning air was crystal clear and cool, and he forgot about business in the elation of riding along with the scent of the forest in the breeze ruffling his hair. He smiled at Gus. The breeze would ruffle her hair, too, if it wasn't held down by that bright yellow hard hat.

Gus caught Cash's smile out of the corner of her eye, and she clenched her jaw. What did he have to grin about? Wasn't he catching on yet to the harsh reality of running a logging operation? If he thought the company had a fat bank account just ripe for the plucking, he was sadly mistaken.

She scowled at the road ahead. He'd mentioned the financial statements, and if he believed their figures, which he should as they were completely accurate, he had to know the company was cash poor.

He wasn't here to skim off cash, she intuitively concluded with a sinking sensation. He was here to stick his nose into the operation, to question and undermine her authority, probably to pronounce himself king of the hill at the first opportunity.

She would die before giving him that chance, she vowed grimly. No damned Saxon had the right to show up after fourteen years and expect a Parrish to bow down three times. Her father would never have stood for it, and neither would she.

Gus turned the pickup onto a crude, rough stretch of road. "The crew is working just ahead," she said stiffly after a few minutes.

Gus sent Cash to the cookhouse to eat dinner with the men. She, in turn, avoided the camaraderie of the evening meal by taking a plate of food from the kitchen to her own house and eating alone.

The day had been a dismal failure as far as discouraging Cash went. He'd been as annoyingly cheerful after tramping through the woods all day as he'd been earlier that morning. Gus realized that he wasn't at all dense, unfortunately. In fact, he grasped fundamentals much too quickly in Gus's estimation. She had shown him areas that had been logged in the past, just to make sure he understood that clear-cutting any portion of this mountain wasn't an option for the company. The new growth in those areas, and the natural maturation of the trees deliberately left untouched five to ten years ago had thrilled the man.

Well, it thrilled her, too, but visualizing herself dealing with Cash for the next five or ten years had been chilling, as well. As for her little ploy with the office machines, she could only grimace in self-disgust and gear up for the day when she would have to face Cash with the more efficient equipment.

One thing was certain: He wasn't going to vanish in the immediate future. Putting Cash to work was her next step, Gus decided while rinsing her plate at her kitchen sink. Maybe a few days of hard labor, sweat and grime would take the starch out of him. Some hard work would take the creases out of his expensive jeans, at least.

As darkness fell, the lighted apartment windows in the office building were all too apparent. Every time Gus got close enough to one of her own windows to notice, her stomach got a little tighter.

Then someone rapped on her front door. After a shower she had donned her nightgown and robe, and she tied the robe's sash tighter as her mouth thinned. Rarely did any of the men knock on her door after dark. Her visitor had to be Cash.

She let him knock a second time and finally yanked the door open with a disgruntled expression. "Yes?"

Cash noticed the robe at once. Pink and pretty, it made Gus Parrish look about sixteen years old.

"Oh," he said. "Guess you're getting ready for bed."

"What did you want?"

"I have some questions, but they can wait till morning."

"Questions about what?"

"About the business. They can wait, Gus."

He had asked questions all day, and she hadn't evaded or dodged very many of them, though she was guilty of emphasizing every negative aspect of the operation and downplaying the positive. It was persistently irritating that he was forming his own opinions rather than relying on hers.

But knowing there were more questions forming in his meddlesome brain made Gus uneasy. She figured it was better to deal with them now rather than spend the night worrying about them.

"Come on in," she said grudgingly, and stepped back for him to do so.

Passing her, Cash caught her clean soapy scent. It was, surprisingly, more arousing than any perfume he'd ever smelled on a woman. Her hair looked slightly damp, he saw after turning around to face her while she closed the door. It was brushed back over her ears and fluffy on top, a style that fit this petite woman to a T.

"Sit down," Gus stated.

"Thanks." Cash went to the same chair he'd used last night. Again his gaze moved around the room. He'd like to see the rest of this appealing log house, he thought.

But not tonight. "I'd like to go over the current production reports in the morning," he said. "Do you have any objection to my snooping around the office?"

Gus drew a breath. Her objections would reach the moon if stacked one on the other, but his legal right to the company records wasn't debatable.

"Snoop all you want," she said flatly. "Anything else?"

"Yes." Cash grinned. "Where can I get some boots like yours?"

Gus had suspected his cowboy boots hadn't been comfortable in the woods today. Yet he'd trudged over rocks, fallen trees and through heavy brush without complaining. Something softened within her, and she didn't like the sensation. Cash Saxon wasn't precisely an enemy, but he was close. Certainly he was an opponent of some sort and not a man with whom she should get too complacent. His good looks rang a warning bell even if he wasn't here to usurp her position in the company. That was his goal eventually, Gus was sure, to ultimately take over and run the show.

Her voice contained the frost of her thoughts. "There's a store in Hamilton that sells steel-toed boots."

"And Hamilton is where?"

"Down the mountain and about twenty miles to the south. But let me warn you. That style of boot is costly, about two hundred dollars." Why she mentioned price Gus would never know. With Cash's money he could probably buy out the entire store and not even notice a dent in his bank account.

"Two hundred," Cash repeated slowly. Getting used to a flat wallet was going to take some time. He had shoes in his wardrobe that had cost six, maybe seven times that amount and their usage had been of a frivolous nature. Now, when he needed sensible boots for a sensible reason, he couldn't afford to buy them. Certainly it wouldn't be wise to use the last of his money. The thought of being completely broke was horrifying.

Unless...? He eyed Gus thoughtfully. "Is there any money from the partnership to disburse?"

"I beg your pardon?" His question dumbfounded Gus, making her revise her previous conclusion about Cash not being here to glom onto the company's meager funds.

"I'm talking about profits," Cash clarified. "Are there any profits in the company account to disburse?"

"No, there are not," she said icily.

"Don't get mad," Cash warned. "I had to ask because..." His mouth closed. Admitting near destitution to someone else was difficult, particularly to this feisty little woman. Had he even really admitted it to himself? He wasn't ready to talk about it, he realized. Maybe his brothers were going through the same thing, or maybe they weren't having any trouble relating recent Saxon family history to curious parties. But pride or ego or something wouldn't let him start spilling the facts behind his need for a profitable and successful outcome to this venture.

Gus waited for an explanation, though she could think of none except out and out greed. The man was wealthy—her father had talked about the Saxons' money often—and he probably wanted to rob the company of the little cash it did have.

Cash's next comment and question affirmed her suspicions. "I should get my name on the bank account. Do we bank in Hamilton?"

It was all Gus could do to keep from exploding. *She* signed the checks, and if he was able to, he'd never have to ask about personal disbursements again!

"We bank in Hamilton," she confirmed in a tense, low voice. "But you cannot take money out of the business account for personal usage."

Cash frowned. "Of course not. But my signature should be on the checking account, all the same. I was thinking of setting up a two-signature system, so that we both have to sign the checks."

Startled, Gus stared. "Uh...that would be...fair...I guess." He was a confusing man, talking about profit disbursements one minute and a two-signature checking system the next. What should she believe about him?

Cash stood up. "Maybe I'll drive to Hamilton tomorrow. Would you be free to go along? I doubt that the bank would add my signature to the account without your approval."

Gus felt sick-to-her-stomach defeated. Cash was barreling ahead at full steam. Apparently she wasn't going to be able to get rid of him with exaggerated negativity or the threat of hard work. She was doomed to endure his interference. The life she loved so much was disappearing before her very eyes.

"I'll call the bank," she said numbly while getting to her feet. Her eyes wouldn't quite meet Cash's. "They'll accept your identity if I tell them to do so."

She looked so forlorn Cash almost went to her to offer consolation. He even took a forward step. But then his hands dropped to his sides. Gus was having an awful time accepting him, and he really couldn't fault her attitude. She'd been in complete control for a long time, and he was threatening that control.

Looking at her, so pretty in that pink robe, Cash realized that he'd get a terrific amount of pleasure out of consoling Gus Parrish. Yes, indeed, there wasn't anything he would rather do right now than take this sexy little woman into his arms and . . . comfort her.

Gus wasn't thinking of anything even remotely sexual, and yet, after a few silent moments, with the two of them standing there separately engrossed, she began feeling a strange tingling on her spine. Her eyes darted to his, and the expression she saw in them altered the tingling on her backbone to outright wariness.

He wouldn't dare make a pass! She whirled, sending the long skirt of her robe flying around her ankles. Three steps away she stopped and whirled again. "If you're through staring, I'd like to go to bed!"

Blinking, Cash thought about hot tempers, and Gus's was maybe the quickest and hottest he'd ever witnessed. And all he'd been doing was looking . . . and speculating. If she got this ticked over a mere look, how would she react if he ever acted upon that speculation?

"I'm through," he growled, not bothering to deny the charge, and headed for the door.

Fuming, Gus let him handle his own departure. Cash stopped at the door for a final remark. "Thanks for your time."

She didn't care if her silence was rude, disgusting or anything else. He could take it any way he wished, she thought angrily as the door closed behind him. How dare he look at her as though she were fair game for any man's erotic ideas? Damn him! She despised the ground he walked on, and she would never feel anything but hatred for Cash Saxon, not ever!

So why was she trembling? Hugging her arms around herself, Gus sank onto the sofa. It came to her then, a thought she disliked intensely: Cash Saxon had just made her feel something very female, a completely involuntary response to a simmering male inspection. Who had given him that kind of power over a woman's senses? And why had *his* crude admiration affected her when other men's didn't?

Rising suddenly, Gus stalked off to bed, snapping off lights as she went. Hell would freeze over before she gave

Cash Saxon so much as a warm smile, let alone anything else. Let him look, that's all he'd ever get the chance to do with Gus Parrish!

Cash undressed and went to bed without turning on a light in the apartment. Crooking an arm beneath his head, he thought about the past few minutes. He'd met some interesting women during his thirty-two years, but none quite so interesting as Gus Parrish.

This was going to be some tug of war, he thought dryly. From a purely male-female point of view, Gus was something special. Without their complex business arrangement in the picture, he would do his best to draw Gus's attention. His own attention was already focused, and it might not be easy to keep her from figuring out the sort of libidinous urges she was arousing.

But he didn't doubt that she would put him in his place very fast, should he so much as hint that he'd like to step across that invisible line between a man and an indifferent woman. Gus *was* indifferent, wasn't she? What a challenge, he thought, his eyes narrowing in the dark. Some men would find Gus Parrish too much of a challenge to resist. Surely he wasn't in that predatory category.

A slight grin tipped one corner of Cash's mouth. There was something about that hot-tempered little gal that brought out a man's hunting instincts. He just might be more of a predator than he'd known before coming to this mountain.

Three

Cash got up early, ate breakfast with the logging crew, and immediately went to the office to familiarize himself with the current records of the operation. The balance in the checkbook was disappointing but about what he'd expected from Gus's huffy comments last night. He was deeply involved in facts and figures when Gus walked in around ten.

"Hi," he said with a friendly smile.

"Hello," she said with no smile at all. He was using her desk, the one by the window, the one her father had used, *her* desk, dammit! Stiffly she went to the second desk and sat down. Picking up the telephone, she dialed a number.

Cash conveyed indifference about her call, when in fact he was listening with great interest.

"Henry Shanks, please," Gus said into the phone. "Henry? Gus Parrish. I'm fine, thanks. Everything's going as usual." She shot Cash a brief glance. "Almost as usual. There'll be a man at the bank sometime today, Henry, a Mr. Cash Saxon.

"Yes, he's one of *those* Saxons. Anyway, Henry, he's coming in to add his signature to the bank account and set up a two-signature system on future checks. His and mine, yes. Would you take care of it, please?

"Thanks, Henry, I appreciate it."

There was a bit of small talk with Henry before Gus hung up the phone. Cash kept his eyes on the papers spread out on the desk in front of him and acted as though he hadn't heard a word she'd said.

Not at all fooled by Cash's bland expression, Gus sat back. "It's done. When you go into the bank, ask for Henry Shanks."

Cash looked up and smiled. Gus was all business this morning, having none of his game-playing. "Will do. Thanks. Old Henry must know you real well."

"*Old* Henry is thirty years old," Gus said dryly. "And drives a Corvette."

"Ah, a *young* old friend. Is young Henry married?"

Gus pushed back her chair. "As a matter of fact, he's not." It tickled her that Cash had asked such a telling question, though where he got his gall she would never know. Henry Shanks was indeed an old friend, but certainly nothing more, merely one of the people she'd grown up with who had remained in the area.

"Hey, don't run off," Cash called as Gus headed for the door.

She stopped and turned. "I have work to do. Do you need me for something?"

"Well . . . no. But I wouldn't mind a little conversation."

Gus's stony gaze dropped to the papers on the desk. On *her* desk. "Are you finding everything in order?"

"In very good order. You're an efficient record keeper."

"My father taught me the business."

"Taught you very well, apparently." Cash grinned. "I can almost see you tagging along behind him in the woods as a kid." It was true. In his mind's eye was a tiny little girl with flying red pigtails, struggling to keep up with her father's long strides over hill and dale.

"Your insight is miles off the mark," Gus said coolly. "Dad never let me tag along in the woods as a kid. I didn't get involved until he became ill. Look, I rarely spend time in the office during the week. Weekends are when I pay bills, do payrolls and catch up on the production reports. So you just go ahead with whatever..."

"Weekends?" Cash interjected, getting to his feet. "Do you work seven days a week?"

"Most weeks, yes."

He grinned teasingly. "When do you relax?"

His grin was much too cute, Gus thought with intense annoyance. He probably was accustomed to women turning into simpering morons over that grin. Well, this was one woman who wasn't going to simper over Cash Saxon, no matter how high he turned up the voltage.

"Knowledge of when and how I relax doesn't come within the perimeters of our partnership," she pointed out with her nose in the air.

Her snotty attitude made Cash laugh. "Ah, Gussie, you and I could make some mighty sweet music together."

Her nose came down fast, and her eyes shot sparks of outrage. "Don't hold your breath, Saxon!" Whirling, she was out the door like a shot.

Cash really did laugh then. Gus's short fuse excited him. She made him feel... happy. Yes, that was the word. With Gus, a laugh was usually bubbling within him and just waiting for a chance to erupt. Women didn't usually make Cash want to laugh, but Gus did, and for all the right reasons in his estimation—because she was pretty, and cute, and quick on the comeback. Unquestionably she was bright and dedicated to the company.

Resuming his seat, he wondered about her personal life. Wondered about young, unmarried Henry Shanks and his Corvette. Wondered if she weren't involved with some man, if not banker Shanks. Wondered about a lot of things, where she'd been living before Big Jim's illness brought her back to the mountain, and what she'd been doing during that phase of her life.

Cash wanted to know all about Gus Parrish, and he wanted her to be friendlier with him. The partnership didn't unite them, but rather acted as some sort of deterrent to friendship. How could he pacify Gus's resentment of his intrusion? Time would do it, maybe.

But there was another aspect of their working relationship that bothered him. The information he'd been absorbing about the business wasn't encouraging. The company consistently made a profit, but only a very small one. Apparently Gus was content to work seven days a week for a meager living; he was not. As far as Cash could tell, the company had plodded along at the same slow and steady pace since its inception. There were ways to beef up production and turn larger profits, but he suspected Gus wouldn't take kindly to change.

Maybe they were destined to be on opposing sides, Cash mused, which wasn't at all satisfying. But he'd come here to do something about his future, and the potential of this logging operation had barely been tapped. The foundation for a profitable business was well in place, established years ago by Big Jim. All it would take to put this company impressively into the black were some guts and determination.

Those could be the ingredients needed to breach that wall around Gus, as well, Cash thought with a slow grin.

He got up then, stacked the papers he'd been reading into a neat pile and went outside to his Wagoneer. He may as well drive to Hamilton and get his banking chore out of the way.

Besides, meeting Mr. Henry Shanks seemed like an interesting undertaking.

Gus was surprised by Cash's absence at the supper table that night. She had decided to eat the evening meal with the crew as she had before Cash's appearance, and had braced herself for sitting down with her partner.

However, the supper hour passed without Cash showing his face. Afterward, Gus checked the clearing for his Wagoneer, which was also absent. Apparently he hadn't yet returned from Hamilton, and she wondered why not.

A woman already? she thought caustically, walking toward her house. On the heels of that idea was a discomfort in her midsection, which she instantly denied. Did she care if Cash Saxon had already found some willing woman in the area? Not on a bet!

And yet the discomfort remained, making Gus jittery during her shower. Cash should have been back no later than midafternoon, even if he'd taken the time after that business at the bank to shop for the steel-toed boots he'd mentioned. What else he might be doing in Hamilton escaped her, though she supposed he might have decided to have dinner in town.

Cash was a frivolous person, Gus thought scornfully. He'd wasted his entire day, hanging around the office this morning and then doing heaven knew what in town this afternoon, when he could have been out in the woods with the crew.

Turning off the shower, Gus reached for a towel. Her edginess wasn't only because of Cash's unexplained absence. Another truck had broken down today. Lloyd Simmons, the mechanic, was the busiest employee on the Parrish-Saxon payroll, the only one of the men who racked up overtime hours. The trucks were crucial to the operation, and had to be kept running at whatever cost. Without the trucks, the logs couldn't be hauled from the mountain to the sawmill.

Gus's nightly routine was so ingrained, she could follow it without conscious thought. Supper and shower in varying order, then nightgown and bathrobe, an hour or so of reading, and bedtime. She got up early, she went to bed early; the hours in between kept her hopping, and she was always tired by sundown.

Yawning, Gus got a clean nightgown from her bureau and dropped it over her head. The bedroom felt stuffy, so she opened one window, then the other. The sound of an engine drifted on the cool night air. It had to be Cash finally returning.

Curiosity got the better of Gus. Racing to the front of the house, she stood in the dark and peered out through a living-room window. The Wagoneer's headlights had been left on, apparently to light Cash's way to the apartment. Gus squinted her eyes to see better. He was carrying something, something that squirmed and wriggled.

"What in the world?" Gus mumbled. Was he carrying a dog?

Cash came back outside from the apartment and walked around the Wagoneer to turn off the headlights. Gus's urge was to go see the dog, or whatever it was Cash had brought back to camp, but after his crack about the two of them making sweet music together, he could get the wrong idea about her paying an after-dark call.

But was she worried about anything Cash might think? *He* was the intruder here, not her. She had every right to be nosy about anything that happened in this camp, particularly anything suspicious her partner might be up to.

Making up her mind, Gus rushed back to her bedroom for a robe. With a flashlight in hand, she made her way from the house to the apartment. The night was exceedingly dark, and she glanced skyward to see clouds had rolled in to shroud the moon. Rain was a familiar element in these mountains, she and the crew weren't stopped by wet weather unless it lasted for days and turned everything to mud. Still, no one liked working in heavy rain, and she hoped the area received only a light sprinkling.

Gus rapped on the apartment's outer door with the butt end of the flashlight. Cash opened it with a slightly lifted eyebrow. "Good evening, Miss Parrish."

His amused tone deserved her annoyance, but Gus chose to ignore it. Peering around him, she spotted the dog, who was, unfortunately, at that very moment piddling on the floor. "You brought a puppy here," she stated accusingly.

Cash's grin faded as he spotted the puddle. "Guess he isn't house-trained."

"Obviously." Gus tried to sound disapproving, but the black-and-white puppy was so cute with his floppy ears and big grin, she sounded only pleased. "What's his name?"

"Doodles. Come on in."

Gus stepped in and closed the door. "Doodles is an awful name." Cash had scrambled for a rag to wipe up the puddle, and Gus sank to her knees on the floor to hold the puppy, which eagerly crawled onto her lap and licked her all over her face. "He's adorable," she said, laughing at the pup's antics.

Doodles wasn't the only adorable thing in this drab little apartment, Cash was thinking. Gus looked like a kid on Christmas morning, sitting there with Doodles leaping all over her.

"Where'd you get him?" Gus asked.

"From a kid alongside of the road, just outside of Hamilton. He'd given away the whole litter today. Doodles was the last one. By the way, I had dinner with young Henry Shanks."

Gus's gaze rose sharply. "You had dinner with Henry? Well, you two must certainly have hit it off."

"Guess we did. Henry's a nice guy."

Gus rolled her eyes. The last thing she could have imagined was Henry and Cash becoming friends so quickly. Not that it mattered. If Cash stayed, as he obviously intended, he would have to make some friends in the area.

Still, it irked her that he was claiming friendship with one of *her* friends. Apparently Cash was going to worm his way into every aspect of her life.

Doodles took a nip at her chin, and Gus forgot Henry's disloyalty and laughed with genuine relish. "How do you like your new home, fella?" She glanced up at Cash. "Where will he sleep?"

"I was hoping there'd be a big box around here someplace. Know of one?"

"Um . . . I think there are a few empty boxes in my storage room," Gus said after thinking about it. "If you want to come home with me, we could take a look." She held the pup up and looked into his big brown eyes. "You need a better name than Doodles."

"Changing his name would confuse him," Cash said. "The boy's been calling him Doodles since birth."

"Well . . . guess you'll have to keep that awful name, little buddy," Gus said on a sigh, and set the pup on the floor. She started to get up and saw Cash's hand in front of her nose. "I don't need any help," she declared and proved it by getting up by herself.

Cash laughed and walked to the door. "Do you object to my opening the door for you?"

"You're opening it for yourself, too, aren't you?" Gus retorted.

"Independent little cuss, aren't you?"

"You don't know the half of it." Gus sailed through the open door with Cash on her heels. She switched on the flashlight and directed the beam of light to the ground. "Watch your step."

"Yes, ma'am," Cash said solemnly, though his mouth twitched with silent laughter.

"You find me amusing, don't you?" Gus said resentfully.

"What I find you, Gussie, is exciting."

Gus stopped walking. "I despise that nickname, and I also despise innuendo."

Cash peered down at her in the dark. "Do you despise me, too?"

"I . . ." This was her chance to lay into him, to tell him that, yes, she despised him and his unheralded presence and his overbearing gall in showing up here at all. Phrases like "greenhorn," and "irritant," and "unnecessary trouble," swarmed in her mind while she craned her neck to look up at his face. He was so much taller, so much bigger, broader, more muscular, more . . . everything, and standing next to him, she felt smaller than she was, shorter, punier, and definitely female.

That was the crux of the turmoil he created. He was so damned male, and he kept her aware of her own femaleness. The thought shook her. "I don't despise you, but I don't like you either," she snapped, and took off walking again.

Cash didn't believe her. Instead he felt that persistent laugh welling again. Gus climbed the steps to her porch and

yanked open the front door before Cash could do it. "The
storage room is at the back of the house," she announced
frostily.

"Yes, ma'am."

She shot him a black look, but proceeded through the
house at a fast pace. Cash kept up, though he took the opportunity to look around beyond the log house's living
room. The kitchen was great, with a lot of varnished wood,
white appliances, red-and-white checkered curtains at the
window and a tablecloth of the same fabric.

Gus went through a door and snapped on a light. The
storage room contained everything from cases of canned
goods to carpentry tools, Cash saw as he stepped across the
threshold.

"Let's see," Gus thoughtfully muttered to herself, and
stepped over a stack of old magazines to reach what she
thought might be an empty box.

Cash's gaze had landed on a shelf with a relatively new
electric typewriter and two slim calculators. Ignoring Gus's
efforts with the cardboard box, he went to the shelf and took
a better look at the office machines.

All at once it struck Gus what he was doing, and she spun
around with her mouth open. Completely forgetting that
she'd stashed the better machines in here was utterly stupid. She'd have to come up with some sort of explanation,
before she embarrassed herself unmercifully.

None came to mind, and she watched Cash turn around
very slowly to give her a fishy-eyed stare.

She cleared her throat. "Uh . . . it was only a . . . gag."

"A gag. Well, I'm certainly laughing," Cash drawled
dryly.

But he wasn't, and his opinion of her "gag" was written
all over his face.

Her chin came up. "Take it any way you want. I knew I'd
have to return these to the office when you said you were
staying, so you don't need to look so damned patroniz-
ing."

"Is that how I look? Actually, Gussie, I'm wondering
what other little tricks you might have pulled on me." He

knew now that calling her Gussie raised her blood pressure, but his own was pretty high and he figured what was good for the gander was good for the goose. Or something like that.

Apparently bathrobes were Gus's routine evening costumes, but Cash wasn't so familiar with the practice that the sight of a woman wearing nightclothes went unnoticed. There might be a gown under that flowered green robe, but he'd be willing to bet that's all there was.

He advanced with nothing explicit in mind, though his every nerve was attuned to the deceitful, sexy little woman sharing this cramped storage room. Gus eyed the door, but Cash's long stride suddenly put him between her and it. Her mouth got instantly dry; it was obvious from his expression that the subject of her "gag" hadn't yet been exhausted.

"Go ahead and get it out of your system," she said with as much menace as she could muster. "You're ticked and may as well say so."

"Oh, I don't know if ticked is the right word," Cash said casually, giving the door a kick to close it.

Gus's eyes got as big as saucers. "Why did you close the door?"

"I'm not sure. Just some sort of automatic reaction to a really dumb joke, maybe." Cash moved closer. His right arm snaked out, looping around Gus's waist and yanking her forward. "Then again," he muttered huskily, "I might have been thinking about this."

His mouth descended to hers before Gus could do more than sputter. She wriggled and pushed against him, but she may as well have pushed against the mountain itself for all the good she did. His lips were on hers and they felt permanently bonded, as though he intended the kiss to go on for a good long while.

She decided to endure and then blast him with every foul word she knew when he came up for air. Only, some weird things began happening in her body, crazy things like fiery tingles, and the kind of sexual aches any thinking woman knew were dangerous.

Kissing Gus was making Cash's head spin. His mouth gentled and became coaxing. His hands moved down her back to her sweet little bottom, which he urged forward to better nestle into the cradle of his thighs. Her taste was unique, and holding her was like nothing he'd ever experienced. Her pushing had stopped, he realized. In fact, she was kissing him back, if he was any judge of kisses.

That's exactly what Gus was doing, kissing Cash's warm, smooth mouth, and forgetting that his name was Saxon. Forgetting a great many other things, as well, such as her penchant for staying distanced from the male ego, and that he'd forced this kissing business on her in the first place.

A husky moan built in her throat, and when his tongue slid between her lips and into her mouth, the moan escaped. They both heard it. Cash responded by pulling her closer, nearly lifting her off the floor in the process. Gus responded with a sudden dizzying recognition of what was happening and a gasp of protest.

But the kiss lasted till Cash needed oxygen. His own hands felt like tentacles, he realized in his euphoric daze of intense desire, moving over Gus as though she was his to enjoy. She was much firmer than he'd supposed. She was curvy and warm and...fabulous.

With her mouth free, Gus first sucked in air then began speaking, albeit hoarsely. "Listen, sport, this might be par for the course where you come from, but out here men don't grab women!"

He let her go, almost as quickly as he'd grabbed her. For a moment they merely stared at each other. Gus's knees felt ready to give out, but she stood her ground. Cash was breathing hard, as though he'd just run a mile. Her own breathing was far from normal.

"Do you want an apology?" he questioned thickly.

"Would you mean it?" she spat.

"Uh...no, probably not."

"Then shove your apology up your nose!" Gus pushed past him on her way to the door. "Find your own damned box."

Cash didn't know where she went, but he was suddenly all alone in the storage room. It took a minute for his heartbeat to slow down. Gus was pure dynamite, and he knew he wasn't apt to forget this little session.

And neither would she, Cash suspected. She'd kissed him back, whether or not she wanted to admit it. His mouth curved into a slow-burning smile. Sooner or later there would be a repeat of tonight, only with a much more satisfying conclusion. He couldn't doubt it.

Rummaging around, Cash came up with an empty box. He turned off the light and closed the door to the storage room. Gus was waiting in the kitchen, standing like a prosecuting attorney, her expression just daring him to try something else.

"This'll do," Cash announced, holding up the box.

"Marvelous," Gus drawled in a scathing voice. "Look, I think we'd better get something straight. I have no intention of looking over my shoulder every time the two of us are alone together. Is that clear enough?"

"Aw, Gussie," he teased. "Is that any way to talk to the man of your dreams?"

"Man of my dreams! Are you demented? I don't even like you! No one invited you here, Saxon, and if you left tomorrow no one would miss you."

He grinned. "You would."

"Like hell I would!" she screeched. Her nerves were all but shattered, and this idiot man just kept grinning at her. She tried to calm herself. "Please . . . just go."

"Don't you want to come to my place and help me tuck Doodles in for the night?"

Striving for patience, Gus looked at the ceiling. The most appalling part of this fiasco was her cooperation in the storage room. How could she have kissed him back? Why hadn't she scratched out his eyes when she'd had the chance?

"Guess not," Cash said with a dramatic sigh. "Well, don't worry about Doodles's hurt feelings. I'll tell him you said good-night."

"Just go," Gus repeated crossly.

Cash started away. "Oh, by the way, would you have an old rug or blanket to put in the box? Doodles will need something warm and cuddly to sleep on." He grinned again. "Every living thing needs something warm and cuddly to sleep on. To sleep with."

Gus's eyes snapped. "You think you're just too cute for words, don't you? Well, you're wrong. You irritate me. You irritate me every minute we're together."

"What you call irritation, honey, I call chemistry."

"Oh, give me strength," Gus groaned. Darting around him, she went back into the storage room and came out with an old blanket, which she tossed at him. "Put Doodles on this."

"Thank you, ma'am."

"Go to hell," Gus muttered as he left the kitchen.

"I heard that," Cash called out cheerfully from the living room.

Gus fumed while the front door opened and closed, then hoped he would trip over something in the dark and break his conceited neck!

It was only when Gus was snuggled beneath the covers in her bed that she allowed herself to really remember the incident in the storage room. Her fingertips rose to her mouth, which still seemed to tingle from Cash's kiss. That kiss had been passionate and suggestive, and she shuddered to think what might have happened if she hadn't regained her senses . . . God, he'd touched her all over!

Well, not exactly *all* over, but he'd touched enough of her to know more about her anatomy than he should. He was too bold and a smartass and . . . and despicable.

Just the same, in a burst of complete honesty, Gus couldn't deny that Cash's kiss had been something special. Not that she'd ever let him know she thought so. He already possessed enough conceit for a dozen men. She could only imagine what that bit of information would do to his already puffed-up ego.

Gus groaned aloud. She had to work with him. If the company persevered as she hoped, she might have to work with Cash Saxon for the rest of her life.

What had she ever done to deserve such a cruel fate?

Four

Cash had his troubles with Doodles that night. The pup scratched around in his box and whined and whimpered until Cash got up, bleary-eyed, and brought him to bed with him. Happy at last, Doodles settled down and went to sleep, and so did Cash.

Before breakfast the next morning, Cash strung a length of chicken wire he'd bought around a trio of trees, put food and water in the enclosure and finally Doodles. The puppy looked at him and cocked his head, as though asking what kind of game this was. Cash walked off, and Doodles immediately caught on that he was trapped and began whimpering.

Cash turned and shook his finger. "Stop, Doodles!" The puppy barked playfully, but then his new master walked off again, and he laid down and put his head on his paws.

Keeping the pup safe while he was absent was uppermost in Cash's mind. He couldn't leave Doodles alone in the apartment all day, and heavy equipment intermittently rolled in and out of the compound with drivers intent on their work. There was plenty of room in the chicken-wire enclosure for the puppy to romp and exercise, so there really was no discomfort to his confinement. Later on, when Doodles was less excitable, Cash figured on taking him where he went, even to the woods.

The woods was Cash's destination for the day. He was eating breakfast with the crew when Gus came in. Mandy served the meals buffet style, lining everything up on a counter in the dining room, where the men helped themselves. Gus took a bowl of oatmeal, a cup of coffee and a cinnamon roll, and then chose a table some distance away from the one Cash was occupying.

He smiled and nodded. She merely nodded.

On the way out afterward, she caught up with him. "What are your plans for the day?"

"I'm going to the woods with the men." He grinned. "What are *your* plans for the day?"

"Work, as usual." Her voice was cool. "You can ride the bus with the men or take your own vehicle. It would probably be wise to drive yourself, in case you want to come back early."

"Why would I want to come back early?"

"Are you accustomed to a long day of hard work?"

Cash refused to get ruffled, though he suspected that was what Gus was hoping to accomplish. "No, but I'm not going to learn the business hanging around here." He looked her right in the eye. "I didn't get much sleep last night. How about you?"

Gus's cheeks got pink, because she knew exactly what he was referring to. "That silly kiss didn't bother me one iota," she scoffed.

"I wasn't talking about that kiss," Cash said with a devilish grin. "Doodles kept me awake."

"You inferred...!" Gus's face got redder, but arguing the point would only dig her embarrassed self into a deeper hole. Her gaze fell on his cowboy boots. "I thought you were going to buy some logging boots."

"Guess I forgot."

He forgot? Gus's embarrassment evolved into conjecture. A lapse of memory seemed like a pretty lame excuse to her, but what other reason could there be for not buying something so necessary to this kind of work?

"You need a hard hat," she stated flatly. "Do you have one?"

"Nope."

Gus looked away. Traditionally the men provided their own hard hats on this job, but if a new employee came along without the financial means to equip himself, the company usually stepped in and helped out.

"There are a few extras in the office," she finally said grudgingly. "In the closet. Help yourself."

The men were climbing into the old ramshackle bus used to transport them to and from the logging site.

"Hold the bus, would you?" Cash asked as he took off running for the office.

Grumbling under her breath, wondering why she would oblige Cash in any way, from offering a hard hat to this trivial chore, she walked over to the door of the bus. "Wait a minute, Mac," she said to the driver. "Cash is riding with you. He'll be right out."

Cash came jogging out of the office with a yellow hard hat under his arm.

"Thanks," he told her as he climbed up into the bus.

"You're welcome, I'm sure," she drawled, though she knew her sarcasm would be drowned out by the rumbling old engine of the bus.

The vehicle lumbered away. Gus's routine was to follow it in her pickup and arrive at the job site at the same time as the men. Today she didn't feel like following. The men would help Cash get started. Undoubtedly the unnerving, highly irritating man had his own ideas about what he'd be doing out there, anyway.

Spotting Doodles within the wire enclosure, Gus crossed the compound and knelt down. The pup practically turned himself inside-out with exuberance. Gus rubbed his wet little nose, scratched his floppy ears and talked nonsense to him.

But then, coming out of nowhere, an urge to cry brought her to her feet. It must be frustration, she thought angrily. Frustration because her hands were tied in the partnership, frustration because Cash always seemed to be one up on her, frustration because she had no next step in mind, and because he'd kissed her last night and she hadn't socked him in the jaw.

No, she had not slept well last night, and yes, it had been because of that distressing kiss. And Cash was a cad for embarrassing her about it this morning. The devil himself lurked in those blue, blue eyes, and all she could do was be on guard against some devious stroke that would cut her completely out of the company.

In a pensive, thoughtful mood, Gus started for the office. There wasn't any legal way for Cash to get rid of her, was there? The Parrish-Saxon partnership was years old, but had anyone ever tested its legality? Was that Cash's true goal here? Why else would a wealthy man move into a rundown apartment and throw himself into a barely profitable business?

Gus's path suddenly veered, and she walked to the apartment's outer door. Glancing around to make sure Mandy wasn't outside to witness her nosiness, she pushed open the door and went in.

The bed was neatly made, surprising her. Cash's scent was in there, she noticed, and found the source in the bathroom—a bottle of very high-priced after-shave. Removing the cap, Gus took a sniff. It was heady stuff, headier still when wafting from a man kissing the living daylights out of a woman.

With her jaw clenched, Gus put down the after-shave and began opening drawers. The usual masculine items greeted her curious eyes, and she closed the drawers and returned to the bedroom. A stack of suitcases filled one corner. Gus opened the closet door and frowned. It was far from filled, and should be crammed if that luggage was any measure. There were jeans, shirts and a couple of jackets on hangers, and several pairs of shoes on the floor.

An inspection of the suitcases told the tale: Cash had barely unpacked.

Gus stood back, suspiciously eyeing the loaded luggage. What did it mean? Wouldn't anyone undergoing a permanent relocation unpack everything? Dare she think his stay wasn't nearly as permanent as he'd indicated? Maybe the reason he hadn't bought those boots was that he wasn't planning to be here long enough to use them.

Grimly Gus surveyed the room again, wishing to God she could read Cash's mind. There was nothing out of place, no papers lying around, no notebooks, no diaries. She walked to the bedstand and picked up the one book on it. It was a spy novel with a marker about one-third through the pages. Sighing, Gus put it down again.

Well, she thought, other than the unpacked suitcases there were no mysteries in here. She shouldn't have snooped, because all she'd gotten out of it was another layer of guilt.

Gus wasn't herself where Cash was concerned. When had she ever gone through another person's things? What had she hoped to find anyway? If he was clever enough to plot some nefarious scheme to steal her half of the company, he was clever enough not to leave evidence lying around.

Of course, she hadn't really gone *through* those suitcases. Maybe under the clothes...?

Gus squared her shoulders. Enough was enough. Honest snooping was one thing; an inch by inch search was something else. Whatever Cash's scheme, she would have to take it as it came.

Leaving the apartment, Gus again made sure Mandy wasn't doing something outside before stepping through the door and pulling it closed.

"Gus?"

Her stomach dropped. Lloyd Simmons, the mechanic, was coming around the back of the building, wiping his hands on a grease rag. She hadn't given Lloyd a thought, and here he'd just caught her coming out of Cash's quarters.

"I need to talk to you about that Kenworth, Gus. Got a minute?"

He appeared not to have noticed what door she'd just come through, Gus realized gratefully. "Sure. What's the problem?"

"The engine in that truck is shot."

"Oh, no," Gus groaned. A diesel engine, even a rebuilt one, cost a fortune. "Lloyd, are you sure?"

"Positive." Lloyd immediately plowed into a lengthy dissertation on the various components of the diesel engine, which Gus just barely understood.

She finally held up her hand. "Stop. I only understand half of what you're saying. Do you know where we can get a rebuilt?"

"Out of Portland, Gus. I called Miller's Equipment Company and they can send one out tomorrow morning." Lloyd added after a moment, "C.O.D., of course."

"Of course," Gus said dryly. "How much?"

"Uh...twelve thousand. It's a darned good price, Gus. Could run up to fifteen."

Gus sighed. Lloyd was right. Twelve thousand was a terrible sum to relinquish, but the engine could have cost more. "All right. Call Miller's again and tell them to..." Cash suddenly flashed into her mind. Decisions of this magnitude could no longer be made unilaterally. Cash would have to cosign the check. Damn!

Her mouth tensed. "Don't do anything right now, Lloyd. I'll get back to you later on."

Gus strode off. Doodles whimpered for attention as she passed his enclosure, but Gus was on a whole other plane of thought. An unexpected twelve thousand dollar expenditure and Cash Saxon's approval on a decision she was perfectly capable of making alone were too much to deal with in the same morning. Hopping into her pickup, Gus headed for the logging site.

Cash's feet were killing him. He'd been a little too eager to get to work, he knew now, insisting on trying out a chain saw and cutting down several of the trees bearing a streak of yellow paint, the method used to denote which trees were ready for harvesting.

Then he'd helped the skidders, the men who cabled the logs and dragged them to the landing via a huge crane. Loading the logs onto a truck had been Cash's next lesson, and he'd been fascinated by the expertise of the men doing the loading.

By then he'd noticed the blisters. Every step had become painful. He wanted to sit down and yank off his boots, but he knew if he did, he wouldn't get them back on again today.

The day felt like a hundred hours long. He had to buy those heavy work boots, even if it took his last dollar. Either that or stay out of the woods.

When Gus's pickup pulled in, Cash nearly whooped with joy. He wasn't thrilled about admitting defeat on his first day in the woods, but he'd rather look like a wimp than permanently maim himself.

He hobbled over to the pickup as Gus got out. She was so engrossed in her own thoughts, she didn't notice Cash's cautious pace. "We need to talk about something."

"We do?" Cash was so glad to see a ride back to camp in his immediate future that he nearly hugged her. Of course, he'd have to do some explaining to get her to drive him back.

Unwittingly Gus helped him out. "Do you want to talk here, or go back to the office? Maybe we should go back. Would you mind?"

Cash offered an understanding smile, though Gus's distracted and obviously worried mood was completely beyond his ken. "Wouldn't mind at all," he said generously.

"Get in then."

Cash waved at the men. "Gotta go back, boys. See you later."

Gus drove with her eyes on the road. Cash could feel her tension in his own system. Whatever was bothering her had to be serious. He braced himself for bad news. "What's wrong, Gus?"

"The Kenworth needs a new engine."

Relieved, Cash sat back. "God, I thought someone had died."

She shot him a venomous look. "Don't start with the cracks. Do you think diesel engines grow on trees?"

He laughed. "Speaking of cracks..."

"I wasn't trying to be funny!"

"Right." Cash cleared his throat and glanced down at his not-so-shiny-anymore cowboy boots, which he'd give almost anything to be rid of. "If the Kenworth needs a new engine, guess we'll just have to buy one."

"It will take the bank account down to practically nothing," Gus said gloomily.

Remembering the balance, Cash gave her a sharp look. "That much?"

"There's money coming in," Gus said, as though reassuring herself. "The company is never completely broke, just very close."

Cash stared out the side window. Something was terribly wrong with an operation that consistently functioned on the brink of bankruptcy. After fourteen years the company should, at the very least, have a cash reserve for emergencies.

"Gus, we need to change policy," he said matter-of-factly.

"We need to change what?"

"Maybe policy isn't the right word, but something needs changing in this outfit."

Gus's temper snapped. "And you're an expert on the logging business? Give me a break, Cash. You've been here for less than a week, and you've already decided what I've been doing wrong? My father, as well? The company's policies are *his* policies, and they've worked for fourteen years. I'll tell you something. There've been dozens of logging companies start up and fail in the Hamilton area during those fourteen years, and this one is still operating. That says something for Dad's policies, don't you think?"

"It says a lot, Gus, but so does the company bank account."

"Listen, you egotistical know-it-all, my dad was the best logger in Oregon! Ask anyone. Go to Hamilton and walk up and down any street. Stop strangers and ask them. They'll tell you what kind of logger Big Jim Parrish was. They'll tell you what kind of man he was. They'll—"

"Stop the truck, Gus."

"I most certainly will not!"

Cash reached out and turned off the ignition. While the truck jerked to a halt, he pocketed the keys. Gus stared at him in disbelief. "What did you do that for?"

"We're going to talk."

"I can talk and drive at the same time!"

"I'm tired of your lecture. Just shut up and listen." Cash turned in the seat to face her. "I'm not denigrating your father. I'm sure he was the best logger, the best father, the best neighbor, the best anything you want to name. But there's something wrong with this company, and in trying to figure out what it is I am not trying to take anything away from Big Jim Parrish.

"Gus, I'm not here to make a hundred bucks a week, or even a thousand. My future is here, and if you weren't so damned bullheaded, you'd know that so is yours."

"Don't be absurd! Of course my future is here. Do you think I'm stupid?" *His* future was here? Gus believed he needed income from this operation just about as much as she believed he could fly. There was always something behind his words that confused her, and what else could it be but a sneaky plan to...to...? Well, she might not know what the plan was, but it certainly wasn't going to do her any good.

"You're the least stupid person I know," Cash said quietly. "But you're also not very imaginative about business."

"And you are," Gus sneered.

"Yes, I think I am. I didn't know that before I got here, but, yes, I think I just might have a head for business. I intend to find out."

"At my expense."

"I'd like our success to be a mutual effort, but I'm going to win even without your cooperation."

"I'm one-half of this partnership," Gus sputtered. "You can't do one single thing without my okay."

"And you can't do anything without mine," Cash retorted. "Do you realize I could shut the entire operation down today merely by refusing to sign those men's paychecks?" It was big talk for a man who barely possessed the price of a pair of work boots, but something had to change or he would never have any more than he had right now. Yes, he would eat, and there would always be a roof over his head, but food and a roof weren't enough. He didn't yearn for riches, he knew, or a soft life. He'd had those things, and they weren't so great.

But satisfaction with oneself was, and maybe that was what he was hoping to gain with the success of this company.

From Gus's shocked expression he knew he'd delivered a nearly fatal blow. "Don't worry. I'm not going to shut it down," he told her. "But neither are you going to stop me from moving forward."

Gus could barely speak. "Give...me the keys," she whispered. She'd known all along that Cash was capable of something like this; she just hadn't known exactly what the "something" was.

"Don't look so damned forlorn," he said softly. "Gus, I'm not trying to hurt you."

"Yeah, right," she mumbled.

"I'm not! Can you honestly say you're totally content with the company as it is now? Weren't you worried sick about buying that engine a few minutes ago? Wouldn't you appreciate fewer worries over money?"

And then comprehension struck Gus. It was astounding, and frightening. She turned her face to him. "You're planning to put money into the company and make it into something huge, aren't you?"

Cash was dumbfounded. Before he could come up with a reply, Gus demanded, "Give me those keys, damn you! If you think I'm going to stand by while you destroy this mountain and this company, you've got another think coming!" She crumpled then, visualizing a clear-cut, denuded mountain, and a voracious company in which she had no say at all. Her hands covered her face. "Oh, why did you ever come here? Why didn't you stay in your own greedy, arrogant realm?''

She was crying. It took Cash a minute, but her teary voice finally sunk in. He slid across the seat. "Gus, you're wrong." He tried to pull her hands away from her face.

"Don't touch me!"

"Listen to me. You're dead wrong about my plans. I don't even have any plans yet." She looked so small, and he felt like the worst kind of jerk. "Gus, please talk to me."

She dropped her hands. He could see her red eyes. "Give me the keys," she said stiffly.

"In a minute."

She gritted her teeth and turned her face to the side window. He was much too close. His thigh was crowding hers. She could smell his sweat, and that costly after-shave.

"We will never agree on company policy," she said dully. "I like it small and you're thinking big. I've wondered why you came here, but it never occurred to me you might be contemplating expansion."

Expansion. The word struck Cash right between the eyes. That's precisely what was needed—newer equipment, lower operating costs, maybe increased production. His pulse began racing.

"That's it," he admitted, speaking to himself as much as her. Expansion. The Parrishes had been trying to operate at one particular level, and even a novice to business knew that standing still was impossible. One either went forward or backward. "Gus, you'll prosper right along with me."

"And nothing will be the same."

"I hope you're right," Cash said passionately.

Her face came around slowly. The second their eyes made contact, she wished she hadn't looked at him at all. Excitement poured from his gaze, and she couldn't tell if it was because of his rapacious plans for the company's future or because they were alone out here.

His hand came up to brush tears from her cheeks. "Do you know how beautiful you are?" he whispered. "I won't hurt you, Gussie, that's a promise."

He'd spoken the loathesome nickname like a caress. Certainly the fingertips on Gus's face were a caress. Her anger was evolving into something bearable, though she didn't know why. Cash was exactly the threat she'd supposed him to be at their initial meeting, and sitting here and allowing him to dry her tears was as traitorous to her own goals as anything could ever be.

Yet her fight seemed to be draining away. His touch was mesmerizing, as was the sensual light in his eyes. She felt herself being emotionally drawn to him. His handsome face came closer. A kiss was imminent, and she did nothing to prevent it from happening.

His lips brushed hers in the gentlest way possible, and the contact felt comforting to her. Comforting and more. Much more. A delicious languor spread through her. Like last night, intimacy made her forget who he really was, and why he was here. Oh, she knew, but the knowledge lost its sharp edges when he touched her. When he kissed her.

He put his hands on her shoulders and turned her toward him, just a little, just so he could kiss her from a more satisfying angle. His mouth teased hers briefly, then settled upon it for a real kiss. He felt her lips part and cling to his, and his hands were no longer steady.

"Gus," he whispered, and brought her closer. She responded by snuggling against him. The heat rose between them. Their kiss became hungry, and passionate, and this time she didn't pull away when his tongue slid into her mouth. Instead her tongue met his, and suddenly, stunningly, they were writhing together to seek a more gratifying position.

Cash managed it. He pulled Gus across his lap, and kissed her again and again. Neither was thinking of business. The excitement of tasting each other, holding each other, was mounting, making them tremble and need more than was practical in the front seat of a pickup, in broad daylight, and while wearing so many clothes.

Groping caresses were exchanged despite the clothes. Right through her shirt and jeans Gus felt the heat of his hands on her body. Her mood took a decided downswing.

This was not a kid's game. They weren't teenagers stealing kisses away from adult eyes. Cash's desire was a man's desire. His arousal was obvious against her backside, her own was an internal torment.

She felt nearly queasy from the desire, utterly defeated. She could feel every spot on her body that touched his, and the sensation weakened her. She was such easy pickings for this man, it was sickening.

Her body sagged, just drooped against him, and she buried her face in his shirt. Cash put his head back and sucked in air. Gus had turned off on him, when he would have continued to fulfillment, some way, somehow.

"What's wrong, baby?" he whispered raggedly.

She sat up, inadvertently grinding her bottom into Cash's lap and missing his responsive wince. "Don't call me baby, though it's probably no more than I deserve."

"What's that supposed to mean?"

"What do you think it means? Have you ever known an easier woman?"

"What?" Cash grabbed her by the shoulders. "Don't put yourself in that category! I haven't and I never will."

Their gazes tangled. "You're a taker, Cash. You want the company, so you take it. You want me, so you take me. Let me ask you something. If you had to make a choice between the company and me, which would you choose?"

He grinned. "Right this minute?"

"Don't be so damned flip. Everything's funny to you, isn't it? This is my life and you're laughing about it. I don't appreciate it, not one little bit."

"Gus, I'm not laughing at you. You make me happy." He peered down at her. "But I don't make you happy, do I?"

"Do you want me to lie about it?"

"Gus, I'm not going to go away."

"You think I don't know that?" Gus scooted to the driver's seat. "Please give me the keys."

Cash dug into his jeans pocket, which was no easy feat considering how full they were, and came out with the keys. He passed them to her waiting hand. Gus immediately started the truck and got it moving.

"What about the engine?" she asked dully, so shaken by the past few minutes she could barely think.

A truck without an engine would have very little trade-in value. "I vote to buy it," Cash told her. His imagination was taking wings. New equipment, or newer than they had, would take money. Would Henry Shanks help out with a bank loan?

He glanced at Gus and wished she were receptive to an unbiased discussion about the company. His wishes went further, encompassing the two of them. She reached him as no other woman ever had, but would she believe him if he said so? She didn't trust him and maybe never would.

Cash's eyes narrowed. There had to be a reason for so much mistrust. Had some guy hurt her and now she didn't trust any man? Or was his own ego getting in the way of a much harsher truth: The company was all that mattered to her, and she'd had it her own way too long to share it now.

He just didn't know. Did Gus even know?

They arrived at the compound. Gus put the pickup in Park and turned off the ignition. "Apparently you're going to make a pass every chance you get," she said tonelessly, then looked at him. "Is that what I should expect from you? Please tell me the truth."

Her candor was a little embarrassing for Cash, but he concealed it and returned her gaze. "You're a sexy woman, Gus."

"And that's all the incentive you need?"

Cash felt his face getting warm. "Not usually, no."

"Then may I ask why you feel you have the right to kiss me whenever the notion strikes?"

She was the one insisting on this conversation, Cash told himself in defense of the only answer he could give her. "I don't kiss you every time I get the notion. If that were the case, we'd be in bed right this minute."

"Oh, really. Cash, I was married once. It was a miserable relationship and lasted only two years. I blamed him, he blamed me. The truth was, I couldn't deal with his monumental ego, and I'm not sure whose fault that was, his or mine. It's not the point, anyway. The point is that I was contented living without a man before you came along, and I would be contented again if you left today. Don't push me into something I'm not ready for. I'm worried that you could do it, and I don't think either one of us would end up very happy."

He drew in a long, slow breath. So that was her background, an unhappy marriage. Still, what did it have to do with the two of them? Surely she wasn't classifying him with an ex-husband who apparently had thought the sun rose and set in his own hind pocket. "You sound awfully positive, Gus. Do you see something wrong with *my* ego?"

Gus got out of the truck, closed the door and looked back in through the open window. "Your ego is alive and thriving, Cash. Believe me, no one could ever accuse you of timidity or a lack of confidence."

"Well, what's wrong with that?" he yelled as she walked away. Gingerly he got out. The soles of his feet felt seared. He'd hiked around in these boots before, and granted they hadn't been all that comfortable. But the moderate discomfort he'd expected from working in them had magnified tenfold.

Mumbling to himself about Gus's confusing attitude, Cash headed for the apartment. He couldn't do another thing until he soaked his feet.

Gus stood at a window in the cookshack and watched him limping along like an old man. "What in the world...?" The problem dawned on her. His boots!

She shook her head in dismay, admitting for the hundredth time that she would never understand Cash Saxon and she may as well stop trying.

Five

On Saturday Gus buried herself in the company records in the office, as was her normal procedure. The logging crew left the mountain on weekends, Mandy as well. The only employee working and staying in camp was Lloyd, who was installing the rebuilt engine in the Kenworth.

Usually Gus enjoyed the quiet weekends. The place without activity was conducive to mental endeavors, and normally she breezed through the book work with few hitches. Today she was much too aware of Cash's presence to concentrate, and she kept losing her train of thought.

Not that he was deliberately bothering her. But she found herself staring out the window when he passed by with Doodles at his heels. He was wearing what appeared to be house slippers, and went into the shop, undoubtedly to check with Lloyd on the progress of the Kenworth. After about fifteen minutes he came out again. But then he just stood there with his hands on his hips and looked off into the distance, as though weighing a matter of great import.

Gus felt a stirring of her senses. Even from across the compound Cash was an imposing figure. *You never have denied his good looks,* she told herself in defense of her admiration for his height and lean build. Why wouldn't she appreciate good looks? She might prefer living without a man at the present, but she wasn't brain-dead.

Neither was she cell-dead, Gus thought with a deep frown. She had heard of explosive passion between a man and a woman, but it hadn't happened to her before. Had she handled the situation well enough? Giving Cash a brief summary of her past had seemed logical at the time, but today the explanation seemed weak and even inaccurate. Larry's massive ego had certainly contributed to their divorce, but wasn't the truth closer to their lack of passion for each other? Sex had been so humdrum as to be boring for both of them. Maybe they'd known it right away and had just hung on for those two years, Gus mused, wondering if she wasn't seeing her marriage in its actual light for the first time.

Regardless, responding to Cash was a dangerous mistake. Everything she had in the world was right here on this mountain. She feared that Cash could outthink her, that he was smarter and more clever in business. Her business experience began and ended with this simple record-keeping, and with the lessons and advice her father had given her during his illness. She understood the mechanics of the operation very well, she had confidence in dealing with the logging crew, and she had never been afraid for the future until Cash showed up. Now a knot of anxiety for the company lay in her stomach and kept her constantly on edge, and the whole awful situation was worsened by personal distress because Cash kept making passes that she not only allowed but returned.

Wondering where her willpower had disappeared to, Gus sighed despondently and picked up her pencil. At this rate, she wouldn't get anything done all weekend.

The rain that had been threatening for two days was going to be a certainty very soon, Cash thought with a glance at the dark and cloudy sky. In fact... He held out his hand, palm up, and felt the moisture of tiny raindrops.

"Hey, Doodles," he said with a laugh. "Do you want to play in the rain, or get under cover?"

The pup bounced around, obviously not caring what he did as long as he was with his master.

Taking that boy's last puppy had been an impulse for Cash, but a dog seemed to fit his new life-style and the squirming little pup had wormed his way into Cash's heart at first sight. In a few months Doodles would be a great companion, he figured, and everything he did these days was for the long haul.

It was a good feeling to be thinking of the long-term, Cash decided while starting for the office building. He knew where he'd be next year and five years down the road. There was a stability here he'd never encountered before, and he liked that idea.

Cash held the door open for Doodles to go in, then he followed. Gus barely looked up. "It's raining," he announced.

Gus glanced out the window. "So it is."

She was using his desk, Cash saw, the one by the window. "Working on the books?"

It was perfectly obvious what she was doing, Gus thought peevishly. "Trying to," she replied pointedly.

Cash laughed softly. "I'm interrupting, right?"

Gus laid down her pencil. "Is there something you want?"

A whole slew of "wants" appeared in Cash's head, most of them revolving around Gus. Rain on the roof, a lazy day? Yeah, he could think of several things he'd like to have right now.

"How about joining me for supper in town?" He tossed out the words casually.

"No, thanks."

"Aw, come on, Gus. You deserve a night out. You worked hard all week."

"You didn't," she said coolly.

Cash's eyes widened. "The lady is capable of low blows."

"Well, did you?"

He grinned. "I tried. I'll do better next week, I promise."

Gus flushed. Last week had been his first, and regardless of her animosity, maligning his efforts to his face was probably going too far.

She picked up her pencil. "Leave me be, Cash. I want to get this work out of the way."

"Can I help?"

Her gaze rose sharply from the papers in front of her. "Do you want to help?"

"Sure, why not? I think I understand what you're doing. I've studied past reports till I'm blue in the face. What're you working on right now?" Cash walked around the desk and leaned forward to read over her shoulder.

Gus fought a shiver and tensed instead. "It's the week's production record," she said weakly, almost hoarsely.

Cash leaned closer, bringing his head down to a level with hers. His eyes were on the report, and he mumbled figures from the work that barely registered in his mind. Gus's scent had him mesmerized, and he was suddenly so focused on the sexy little woman practically in his arms, she could have been computing the national debt and he wouldn't have known it.

He honestly couldn't move away from her, though Gus was squeezing against the opposite side of her chair to avoid contact with him. She was wearing a bright blue sweater with short sleeves today, and that sweater seemed spun of some soft, magical yarn that just begged Cash to touch it. He could look down and see the swells of her breasts. Her hair smelled of something slightly fruity, and he was positive he could even smell the light coating of lipstick on her sensuous lips.

His mind was spinning, his body was aching, and without thinking about consequences or anything else, he tipped Gus's chin with his forefinger and looked into her eyes, which were wide and startled.

"Don't..." she whispered. "I asked you not to...." But her own mind was spinning as fast as Cash's, and him standing over her with his heat and sexy after-shave had destroyed her every resolve to stay far, far out of his reach.

"Gus, something important is happening with us," he said huskily.

"No...I...Cash..." She couldn't form a coherent thought. His face was two inches from hers, with his one hand holding her chin and the other on the arm of her chair.

He kissed her. He placed his mouth on hers and kissed her, and in the back of Gus's dazed mind was the realization that she'd been hoping he would. Telling herself otherwise, insisting she wanted nothing to do with Cash was self-delusion. What she wanted was making her dizzy, and making her lips move beneath his, stealing her breath and giving her body the shakes.

The kiss deepened, changing from tentative and a little uncertain to demanding and lustful. The hunger between them had them both seeing stars. Cash pulled Gus's chair away from the desk and turned it to face him. Then he took her hands and brought her to her feet. He scooped her into a fierce embrace and possessed her lips again, and this kiss conveyed all of the pent-up desire he'd been battling since their first meeting.

It was overwhelming for Gus. She caught herself moving her body against his, rubbing her breasts against his chest and plunging her tongue into his mouth. Her arms were around his waist, uniting them in the closest way possible with her standing on tiptoes and him trying to be shorter than his six-foot-one-inch height. He wasn't asking and she wasn't giving permission, and yet they were functioning on the same wavelength, needing each other with an almost frantic desperation.

When was no longer a question in Cash's mind, but *where* was. Her house or his apartment. The office wasn't an option, as Lloyd could come strolling in without warning. There was a connecting door with the apartment, and Cash took a second to eye it and make his decision. Then he bent over and lifted Gus off the floor and into his arms.

With her hands up around his neck, Gus whimpered into his throat while he carried her to the door. The word *mis-*

take drifted through her mind. She shouldn't be doing this, but she wanted it so much. Never had she wanted a man the way she wanted Cash. Her body was on fire from the wanting. This had nothing to do with the company, she assured herself, nothing to do with love. This was merely her own need to experience true passion just once in her life.

Cash managed to open the door. Gus wasn't heavy, no more than a hundred pounds, he figured, and in his present state of arousal he could have carried three times that weight. Closing the door again was a little tougher, but he managed that, too, and even turned the lock just in case Lloyd should come looking for him. He wanted no interruptions for the next few hours, maybe for longer than that.

Aware that Doodles had made it through the door as well, Cash brought Gus to the bed and sat down with her on his lap. "Look at me, Gus," he whispered.

She took her face out of his throat and opened her eyes. There were no objections, no denials, no refusals in them, and he smiled, a slow, completely sexual smile that made Gus realize how hot the fire was that she was playing with. Perversely, it also made her want him more.

She licked her lips and saw the flames rise higher in his eyes. He slowly slid a hand under her sweater and to her breast. Her bra was confining, but he cupped the firm flesh and felt her nipple responding through the fabric.

Gus undid the top button on his shirt. "Do it," he whispered raggedly. "Open them all." Holding and caressing her breasts was better than he'd imagined, just as he suspected having all of her was going to be. "You're beautiful, Gus," he said as his gaze moved over the features of her face. "I love your hair."

"I...kind of...love yours, too," she said unsteadily, and lifted her hands to run her fingers through his thick, coarse hair.

He laughed softly. "I love your freckles."

"You couldn't," she whispered, aghast that he would even mention her accursed freckles.

"But I do." He raised her sweater and pressed his mouth to the cleavage between the cups of her bra. "I love your breasts."

She could barely breathe, and stopped entirely when his tongue flicked against her skin. He left her chest to kiss her lips, and her responsive moan sounded suspiciously like a sob.

The sounds they made amplified their desire. Cash's heavy breathing heightened Gus's desire, and the tiny whimpers and gasps she made heightened Cash's. He'd never felt so in tune with a woman before. This wasn't just an ordinary burst of passion for him, though he could only wonder what it was for Gus. Certainly she needed what he did. Her small body kept arching and writhing against his, and her mouth was almost greedy in its hunger.

He suddenly needed her naked, needed to be naked himself. "Let's get rid of these clothes," he whispered, and worked the blue sweater up and over her head. It mussed her hair, but neither noticed. Cash was intent on unhooking her bra, and Gus was sliding the shirt from his broad shoulders.

Naked to the waist, they looked at each other, basking in the beauty each saw. "Damn, Gus," he whispered raggedly. Her body was perfection, her nipples especially. Full, tight and a rich rose color, they pointed directly at him.

The word *perfection* hadn't escaped Gus's thoughts, either. A man's chest had never thrilled her all that much, but Cash's did. His belly was flat and hard, and his muscles, though not overly exaggerated, were pure male. There was one small triangular patch of hair between his nipples, and the rest of his skin was dark and as smooth as glass.

"You have a tan," she said softly.

"You don't," he said thickly, gazing adoringly at her milky-white skin. His hands rose to her breasts, one on each. "Gus, I love..." He stopped, because there was so much about her to love, he wondered if he wouldn't go too far.

He palmed her nipples to rigidity, and watched Gus close her eyes to savor the sensation. That was all he could take.

Having her on his lap bearing down on his straining fly was more torment than he could handle.

He brought them both to the bed, placing Gus on her back. There was no more talk. He kissed her hard and thoroughly for a very long time, then sat up to remove her jeans.

She spoke in a shaky, low voice. "Is the door locked?"

"One of them is," Cash replied grimly. Even this minor interruption was too much, but he got off the bed and locked the outside door. When he turned around, Gus was under the covers. He spotted her jeans and panties on the floor.

He walked to the bed and unbuckled his belt. Gus averted her eyes. "Don't look away," he said gruffly.

Her head turned on the pillow, and her gaze rose to his face. He wanted so much, maybe more than she could give.

Cash kicked off his shoes, pulled off his socks, unzipped his jeans and dragged them down his hips, taking his shorts with them. It bothered him that Gus wouldn't look below his chin, but she was in his bed and waiting for him, and maybe he shouldn't create problems where there were none.

Under the covers with her, he pulled her into his arms. "Are you having second thoughts?" he whispered with his mouth in her hair. If she was, he might expire on the spot. He was so ready to make love he hurt.

"I . . . don't know. Kiss me."

He complied, gladly, and immediately felt a renewal of Gus's desire. Her mouth was the sweetest he'd ever tasted, her body the most arousing he'd ever touched. He spent delicious minutes in ardent kissing and a detailed exploration of her breasts.

Then his hand skimmed down her belly. The hair between her legs felt silky soft. He pressed his arousal into her hip and couldn't stop himself from rubbing against her.

Gus was light-headed and completely mesmerized. Cash Saxon knew how to kiss, and how to arouse. No one could know any more than he did. His fingers between her legs were making her crazy. She couldn't lie still.

"Do you have protection?" she gasped.

"I'll take care of it." He did, quickly, as though the condom had materialized at the appropriate moment all on its own.

Gus welcomed his penetration with a sob of intense pleasure. Never had she felt anything like what she was feeling beneath Cash. If this was what people were supposed to feel, no wonder she and Larry had been bored in bed. And how could that sort of boredom not spill over into a couple's daily life?

The wild and pleasurable peak nearly caused Gus to black out. Now she knew, she thought through a pink haze of supreme satisfaction. How could a woman live twenty-eight years and completely miss this moment?

Coming down was almost as gratifying for Gus as the high point had been. Cash was heavy on her, lying as though dead, but her own system was so mellow and loose, she doubted that anything could disrupt it.

She naively thought that, until reality returned. Her gaze moved beyond Cash's head to the drab walls of the apartment. She was in his bed, lying under him, lying under a man she'd be a fool to trust.

Her heart sank as all remnants of passion vanished. It was over. She'd experienced what she'd been driven to know, and now it was over.

"I'd like to get up," she bravely announced, not sure how she should deal with the aftermath of such unrestrained behavior.

Cash raised his head. He was wearing a satisfied smile. One look at Gus's face reduced the smile to a mere wisp of its former brilliance. "Uh... something wrong?"

"This..." She didn't know how to explain herself. "This shouldn't have happened," she finally blurted.

One of Cash's eyebrows shot up. "Don't you think it's a little late for that opinion?"

"I had that opinion all along. Didn't I ask you to stay away from me?"

"Pardon me if I missed it, but did you say no a while ago?"

Gus's face flamed. "I should have."

"But you didn't say it. Gus, you're a mighty confusing woman."

"Get off of me."

He was in no hurry to obey. Gus's change of heart was damned disturbing. In their present position, he at least had her full attention.

"Now is when we should be saying nice things to each other," he said softly. "Things like, it was great for me, and how was it for you? It was good, Gussie, wasn't it?" He peered at her with a teasing twinkle in his eyes. "Answer me, Gus. Tell me the truth. Don't spare my feelings. Was it good for you?" He already knew it was, he just wanted to hear her say it.

Yet he wanted more than that. He wanted her to stay in bed with him for the rest of the day. The rain on the roof was lulling. Doodles was quiet, probably sleeping. Lloyd might even have gone, as he'd told Cash he was only planning to work another hour or so and then he'd be heading down the mountain to spend the night with his wife and kids. He'd added that he'd be back in the morning to finish up the Kenworth's repairs.

And maybe, Cash mused further, he wanted Gus to talk about commitment. Nothing drastic or binding, merely an acknowledgment of mutual affection and some small thing about today not being just a roll in the hay for either of them.

Gus only wanted to escape. Doing it had been bad enough, talking about liking it was more than she was capable of giving him.

"I'm not going to discuss it," she said stubbornly. "Now, please move so I can get up."

Cash's eyes narrowed, and he wasn't teasing anymore. "Didn't it mean anything to you?"

"Cash, what do you want it to mean? Can't you see you're embarrassing me?"

"Embarrassing you! We just made love. How in hell could talking about it be embarrassing?"

"Another point we don't see eye to eye on," Gus said while turning her head to avoid his accusing gaze.

Cash was getting mad. "You liked it, lady, you liked it a lot!" Gus closed her eyes. "Is that how you deal with problems, just close your eyes and hope they go away? I'm not going to disappear that easily, Gus."

"Don't I know it," Gus mumbled. She felt sick to her stomach. How could she be such a fool? She should have socked him the first time he kissed her. Today she should have gotten out the shotgun!

But, no, she'd melted into some sort of simpering . . .

God, she really *had* simpered, exactly as she'd vowed not to do!

Gus threw her head back and groaned. "Giving you this kind of hold over me is the stupidest thing I could ever have done. I can't even imagine what you'll do with it."

Muttering a curse, Cash rolled to the other side of the bed. Gus sat up and then wondered how she was going to get her clothes without showing him her bare behind.

She groaned again and bent forward to bury her face in the covers on her own lap. The bed heaved as Cash got off of it, and she was relieved to look up and see him vanishing into the bathroom.

Quickly she jumped out of bed and grabbed her jeans and panties. They were tangled together, and her hands shook in her haste to get them separated and on her body before Cash came back.

She was in her panties and fastening her bra when Cash returned stark naked. Startled, she turned her back.

With a grim expression he picked up his jeans and yanked them on, leaving his shorts on the floor. "Let's get one thing clear," he said harshly. "We *both* liked it, you as much as me. A man knows, Gus, and you had one hell of a good time."

"You're crude." She scrambled into her jeans.

"And you're blind! Why do you think this gives me a hold over you? Are you talking about the company? For your information I don't see a connection between the two, and if you do you're one sadly mixed up woman."

Gus jerked the sweater over her head. "You bet I'm mixed up! And who caused it? You, Cash, no one else!

Coming here and throwing your weight around, talking about changing policy, and . . . and Lord knows what else. Let me tell you something, mister. You're not changing one damned thing, not one! And if you try to shut down the operation, I'll sue your butt off! How do you like *those* apples?''

Cash walked over to her and put his face right in hers. "I *will* change things, and neither you nor anyone else is going to stop me! This company is operating in the dark ages, and if you got your screwed-up ideas from your old man, so was he!''

Gus lunged at him with the intention of slapping him silly. Cash caught her by the wrists and laughed, though with more bitterness than humor. "Do you think I'm going to stand still and let a pint-size woman knock me around? Cool down, babe, or you just might find yourself on the floor."

Sweaty and red-faced, they faced each other. There was passion between them again, but not the romantic kind. The air reeked of their anger. "Don't you ever make that kind of crack about my father again," Gus snapped. "I don't care how damned big you are."

"That's mighty brave talk from someone no bigger than a flea," Cash drawled. He had her by the wrists, and she was close enough to kiss.

And that was what he decided to do rather than turn her over his knee. He yanked her forward and into his arms, and when she screeched and jerked her head back and forth to avoid what was coming, he took her chin and forced her face around.

Then his mouth clamped down on hers, hard and rough. It was only when he felt her trembling against him that he stopped the rough stuff. But he kept on kissing her, and enjoying it in the bargain. Damn, she was something, a little spitfire and so sexy he couldn't see straight.

He finally came up for air. Gus's mouth felt swollen and tears were stingingly close, but Cash Saxon wasn't going to see them.

"You won't let yourself believe that I have no intention of hurting you, will you?" Cash questioned. "Gus, today meant something to me. I could make love to you again right now. You're special and—''

"This time I'm saying no, loud and clear. Are you going to force me into that bed again, like you just did with that kiss?''

Cash gave up. Dropping his hands, he stepped back. "Forget I mentioned it. Forget today ever happened. From now on it's strictly business between us, okay? That's what you want, that's what you'll get."

"I pray you mean it," Gus said evenly, and marched to the door.

"Gus, dammit," Cash groaned, and darted to the door to keep her from opening it. Her back was to him, and he nuzzled his face in her hair and pressed his body against hers. "Don't leave like this," he whispered. "Gus, we've got something special. Don't lock it out. You're hurting yourself as much as me.''

Confusion caused her to hesitate. What if he meant every nice thing he'd said? What if all the trouble was only in her own mind? What if he was right and she was wrong?

Her shoulders slumped. "Promise to leave me alone.''

"What?" Cash lifted his head.

"I want you to promise to leave me be," she repeated brokenly. "I'm weak where you're concerned. I don't know why and I'm not even sure I want to know. I need some time to figure things out.''

"Gussie..." He stroked her hair. "It's so simple. We mesh, honey. That's all there is to it. We've got this crazy chemistry, and you're thinking it's wrong when it's not."

"I'm not going to... to make love with you again," she whispered.

Cash laughed softly. "You might feel differently about that in a day or so. I feel differently right now. I could..." God, he could, over and over again. With Gus in his bed, anything was possible.

"I *know* how you feel," Gus interjected with some sarcasm. "You've already made that abundantly clear. But your sexual prowess is not in question here." Gus turned around. "Let me tell you something. I never liked sex."

He wanted to grin, but this didn't seem to be the most favorable moment to display amusement. If Gus didn't like sex, he'd never met a woman who did. He cleared his throat. "I think you liked it a few minutes ago," he pointed out delicately. "But you don't have to talk about it," he hastened to add.

"I don't trust you, Cash," she said bluntly. "And I personally don't give beans about your remarkable ability to separate what happened here today and our business relationship. But my own confusion does concern me, and I need some time to sort it all out. In the meantime, I will not agree to—" she glanced at the bed "—to another session like that one."

"And you want me to promise to keep my distance." His gaze moved down her body to her lush bosom, and down further to the snug jeans delineating her thighs. He'd been between those thighs and the memory would keep him aroused for the next ten years. "All right," he agreed. "Fine. No problem."

"Can I bank on that?"

"My word is my bond," he said solemnly.

Gus could tell he was lying through his pearly-whites. The second her guard was down he'd be all over her!

"You . . . you *rat!*" Whirling, she grabbed the doorknob, finally realized she had to unlock it first, managed that nearly impossible task in her haste to leave, and ultimately left to the infuriating sound of Cash chuckling behind her.

He called out the door. "I may be a rat, sweetheart, but you're my little ratette. I just made up that word. What's the right word for a cute, sexy little female rat, Gussie?"

"Go to hell!" she shouted over her shoulder. "And stay there!"

Six

Gus rapped on her friend Karen's front door. It opened after a minute. "Hi," Gus said, sounding as dismal as she felt.

"Good Lord, you *are* in bad shape. When you called... Come on in. We don't need to talk on the front stoop." Karen Post took the overnight case from Gus's hand and then led her into the house.

"You're sure this isn't an imposition, Karen?"

"No way. Bud's working all weekend and I'm thrilled for the company. Besides, I don't see enough of you, Gus. Come on, we'll put your bag in the guest room."

During the drive to the small coastal town where Karen and Bud had lived since their marriage and move from Hamilton, Gus had worried about her impulsive telephone call. It had taken only a few distraught words to wrangle an overnight invitation out of Karen, and Gus was feeling guilty about it.

But she had also felt an overpowering need to talk to someone, another woman, and Karen was an old friend with a generous nature and a broad mind. Of all the people Gus had grown up with who were still within reach, she felt closest to Karen.

"I just made a pot of tea," Karen announced after the bag had been deposited in the guest room. "Let's get a cup and sit in the family room."

"Your house looks great, Karen. You've been doing some wallpapering," Gus remarked en route to the kitchen.

"We're getting ready for the baby," Karen said with unmistakable pride. "I'm pregnant, Gus."

Gus stopped. "Oh, Karen, that's wonderful." She gave her friend a big hug. Karen and Bud had wanted a child since the early years of their marriage. "I'm so glad for you."

They settled down in the family room with their tea and a plate of homemade cookies. They'd known each other since childhood, and Gus felt a hundred years away from those less stressful days. "When is the baby due?" she asked. "You don't look any different."

"I'm only ten weeks along."

They discussed motherhood and birth until Karen changed the subject. "Gus, tell me what's bothering you."

Gus sighed. Karen's secure life was so vastly different than her own. Karen had a happy, longtime marriage, a beautiful house and a baby on the way. Gus had a divorce in her past, fifty percent of a partnership made in hell and a personal relationship that scared the wits out of her.

It seemed so spineless to lay her problems on Karen's shoulders. "Maybe we shouldn't talk about me."

Karen lifted an eyebrow. "Listen, pal, I've been on pins and needles since you called, and I'm not going to let you get away with evasion. Give, Gus."

Gus had to laugh, albeit briefly. "All right, but you asked for it." She related Cash's startling arrival. "After fourteen years, how could anyone have been prepared for a Saxon just showing up?"

"Had to have been a shock, all right," Karen agreed. "But you always knew there was a partner in the company, Gus."

"Sure, somewhere out there in outer space," Gus said gloomily. "I'm worried sick, Karen. Cash has loads of money. How can I compete with money and more confidence than any one man deserves? He's... overwhelming."

"Sounds like it. What's he done so far?"

"He's been going through records, and he put his name on the bank account, and... and he had dinner with Henry Shanks." Gus groped for more. There had to be more. After all, she wasn't worried without cause. But Karen was frowning, obviously not grasping the gist of her concern. "He's talking about changing policy!" Gus exclaimed as she recalled Cash's worst sin. "He actually said, right to my face, that Dad operated the company in the dark ages. Can you believe such gall?"

"I'm not sure I understand. What policy does he want changed?"

"He wants the company to make more money."

Karen laughed. "Don't tell me you're objecting to more money, Gus."

"Of course not, but his methods..." Gus stopped. Cash hadn't talked about methods, merely goals. Higher profits. "I don't know what he's got in mind," she finally admitted. "But I don't trust him, Karen."

"Hmm." After a pause, Karen casually asked, "How old is he? What does he look like? Is he married?"

Gus became very businesslike. "His looks aren't important. He's around thirty. And he's single."

"Young, single and good-looking? Rich, too?" Karen gave a woman-to-woman laugh. "Sounds like Cash's a good catch, Gus." She took a sip of tea. "Are you sure you're not missing the boat?"

"I don't want anything to do with him!" Gus said vehemently. Her shoulders slumped. "He...he won't take no for an answer."

"Ah," Karen murmured. "And therein lies the real problem." The young women's eyes met. "Are you falling for him, Gus?" Karen asked softly.

"I...don't know," Gus whispered. "He scares me, Karen. He's so... sexual."

Karen leaned forward. "Is that bad?"

"Karen, do you...enjoy sex?"

"I love Bud and, yes, I enjoy sex. What's wrong, Gus?"

Gus drew in a long, slow breath. "I never did. Larry and I...nothing was very good...especially in the bedroom. He's the only man I...well, you know...until..."

"Until Mr. Saxon. And you like it with him and that scares you."

Gus got up to pace. "I shouldn't like *anything* with that man. He's going to destroy the company, I know he is!"

"Intuition, right?" Karen said speculatively.

"Instinct," Gus retorted. "He's always laughing at something I say or do, as though I'm there strictly for his entertainment. He's weird. The other day he came back to camp with a puppy. Said he got it from a kid alongside of the road. Probably one of the Monroe kids. They've always got a litter of puppies or kittens to give away."

Karen nodded. "Definitely weird."

Gus didn't notice the chuckle behind her friend's comment. "He's smart, Karen, smarter than I am about business. Why wouldn't he be, growing up with that kind of money? He probably has the best education money can buy. What do I have? A couple of years of college and Dad's advice."

"You're smart, too, Gus, and you've got more guts than any other woman I know. Do you think I would ever tackle a logging operation? No way, pal."

The conversation went on until Bud came home for dinner. Then the three of them sat around and talked about mutual friends and local events till bedtime.

When the house was quiet, Gus stared at the Posts' guest room ceiling and thought about Cash. The biggest question to ponder was why they had ended up in bed together. The second biggest was, would it happen again?

Gus tried to swear it wouldn't, but deep down she wasn't all that certain. Common sense hadn't prevented it from happening today, and what other defense did she have?

Today she'd run away from the problem, but how often could she use that ploy to avoid Cash? She couldn't elude him for long, and she shouldn't be eluding him, anyway. Lord only knew what mischief he might cook up in her absence.

Cash had seen Gus's pickup driving away, but he'd assumed she'd be gone only a short while. As the day got later and then darkness fell, he started to worry. Concerned that maybe her truck had broken down on one of the mountain roads between Hamilton and camp, he got into the Wagoneer and drove to town. Once there, he cruised Hamilton's main streets with an eye peeled for her pickup. It was midnight when he finally got back to the mountain, and he went to bed more than a little on edge.

The first thing he did in the morning was look out the window: Gus's usual parking spot was still empty. She had deliberately gone somewhere for the night and hadn't had the courtesy to say so. From Cash's point of view, Gus was pretty damned selfish, not giving two hoots if he'd put in a restless night listening for her truck and worrying for her safety.

Their relationship was disturbing and getting more so by the day. He couldn't speak honestly to Gus because she wouldn't permit honesty. She had made beautiful, exciting love with him and then let him know she didn't like sex. She was bullheaded about the company and protective of her father every time Cash suggested or even hinted that things could be better.

Drinking coffee in the cookhouse, Cash tried to face the reality of the situation. He could let well enough alone and go along with Gus's methods of running the company, in which case she might relax her guard and let herself like him.

Or he could forget that aspect of their relationship and do what he felt was right, gear this operation up and make it into the successful, profitable business it should be. Although calling a halt to what was developing between him and Gus on a personal level wouldn't be easy. He was closer to an emotional commitment with her than he'd ever been with a woman. Didn't she realize what she was turning her back on? Or didn't she care?

Cash's expression became grimly introspective. Gus was an unknown; this company was not. If he went along with her practices he'd be stuck in a poky little company and eternally worried about money. So would she, but apparently she was willing to accept the discomfort as a matter of course. He was not. The rebuilt engine for the Kenworth was a perfect example. What would happen if two major disasters occurred simultaneously? Or three?

He couldn't do it. He couldn't sit idly by and give Gus a free hand. She was in a rut with the business and he couldn't jump into that same hole and be contented with it, even if it meant the end for the two of them. He didn't like it, but if that's how Gus wanted it, so be it.

After fixing himself some breakfast and doing the dishes after he ate, Cash went to the office and got to work.

Karen walked Gus out to her truck. "Come back again, Gus, soon."

"Thanks for everything, Karen." She stood at the door of the pickup and looked at her friend. "So after listening to my woes for hours on end, what do you think?"

Karen looked away for a moment, then brought her gaze back to Gus. "I think you're falling for Cash Saxon, Gus. I think you're worried about his plans for the company, and you're torn up because you like the guy more than you feel is wise under the circumstances. But I think you should give him a chance. From what you told me, he hasn't done anything to hurt either you or the company. Rather, it sounds to me like he's trying to fit in. Maybe his ideas about policy changes would be beneficial. You talked about financial problems. Maybe Cash's ideas would turn things around and you wouldn't have to worry about money in the future."

Gus nodded and managed a weak smile. "Maybe I've been too judgmental. I keep wondering how Dad would have dealt with the situation."

"Your dad wouldn't be in the same situation, Gus," Karen pointed out with some wryness.

Gus gave a short laugh. "Guess he wouldn't." She hugged her friend. "Thanks again. Tell Bud thanks, too."

"Keep me informed."

"I will."

Gus drove away and headed for home pondering Karen's advice. *Give Cash a chance. Listen to his ideas.* She couldn't dissolve the partnership and Cash was the other half of it. Maybe she had been too judgmental. Certainly she hadn't been receptive to any comment of his regarding change.

For the first time she wondered exactly what changes he had in mind. She would never agree to clear-cutting any portion of the mountain, so if his ideas were merely beefed-up production schedules to make some fast money, they were in for a major battle.

Gus decided to listen to what Cash had to say. The drive home was several hours long, and she finally pulled into camp in a much better frame of mind than the confusion she'd felt yesterday.

From the desk near the window in the office, Cash saw Gus's truck driving in. With an immediately faster heartbeat he got to his feet. Doodles had been romping around the room, and the pup became watchful, prepared to follow should his master suddenly go through the door.

Forgetting the papers in his hand, Cash went outside. Doodles slithered through the opening of the door as slick as a whistle, and managed the stairs to the ground right on his master's heels. Spotting Gus, the pup barked a greeting.

Gus smiled and knelt down to pick up the puppy. "Hey, little buddy, glad to see me?" Doodles wriggled and licked her chin.

Cash spoke coldly. "*I'm* glad to see you're in one piece."

His tone surprised Gus. She sent him a sharp glance. There was none of the laughter in his electric blue eyes she'd come to expect. "Did you think I wasn't?"

"It occurred to me, yes."

His eyes were hard, Gus realized. Maybe he was finally giving her a taste of his true nature. "Not that it's any of *your* business, but I went to visit a friend," she said stiffly while lowering Doodles to the ground. An acute sense of loss was suddenly painful. She reached into the pickup for her overnight case.

Cash took the moment to notice her skirt. Up to now she'd lived in jeans. The denim skirt was fitted at the waist and flared from her hips. Her blouse was white and had a scooped neckline. She was prettier today than she'd ever been. It was all he could do to remember his decision to stay away from her.

Gus gave the pickup door a push to close it. Carrying her overnight case, she started for her house.

"Will you come to the office in a few minutes?" Cash called. "There's a matter we need to discuss."

"I'll be there." Gus wearily threw the words over her shoulder. Cash's unusual coldness had her confused again. She'd arrived home blaming herself for their ill will and prepared for a smoother relationship. Apparently not.

Inside her house, Gus took a few minutes to compose herself. In the bathroom she brushed her hair and studied her reflection. She had always hated being so small. Her father had been a huge man, her mother of an average height. But her maternal grandmother had been a tiny woman. Gus remembered her mother talking about Grandma Kelly's size three feet.

Well, *her* feet weren't a size three, but unquestionably she'd inherited Grandma Kelly's small stature. Her red hair came from Big Jim, another feature Gus wasn't so thrilled with, particularly when her mother had had exceptionally beautiful hair the color of a raven's wing, a poetic description supplied by Big Jim.

Gus barely remembered her mother. Lila Parrish had died the year Gus was six. She'd grown up under her father's care, and would have gladly followed him around in the woods, as Cash had suggested. But Big Jim Parrish had been strictly divided on male and female roles, and to his way of thinking, little girls didn't mingle with loggers. Time had mellowed his old-fashioned ethics, and he'd been only relieved when Gus had come home and willingly taken over the operation.

Sighing, Gus put down her hairbrush. What did Cash want to discuss now? She wasn't in any mood to talk about the business, though she'd been ready to do just that when she got back. Now she didn't know what to think. Certainly she hadn't expected Cash to be so cold and angry. So what had put the knot in his tail, her leaving the mountain, or her leaving without notifying him of her plans? Did he actually believe yesterday gave him some sort of hold on her? Was he one of *those* men, the kind who thought any woman he wanted should snap to attention at his command?

People were returning to camp. Mandy was back, and Lloyd had been working in the shop all day. The place was coming alive, with vehicles arriving and men's voices.

Gus waved a greeting to a couple of the men as she walked to the office. Bracing herself for whatever Cash's subject matter might be, she opened the office door and went in.

Instantly she gritted her teeth. Why did he insist on using her desk? Maybe it was time to clear the air on that point.

Cash was looking at her. "In case you haven't noticed, that's the desk I use when I'm working in here," Gus announced.

"Since you weren't here to use it today, it hardly matters that I did."

"There's nothing wrong with the other one."

Cash took a long look at the second desk. "Doesn't appear to be."

"Don't be purposely irritating! I don't like you using my desk. Is that clear enough?"

Cash folded his arms. "You do enjoy giving orders, don't you? Maybe that's why you resent my being here, because you're not the only authority on the mountain anymore."

Gus didn't deny resentment of his presence, though his sardonic accusation definitely ruffled her feathers. "What did you call me over here to talk about?" she snapped.

Patience, Cash told himself. A fight now would only delay a necessary discussion. "You know Cal Hayden, don't you?"

"He's the manager of the sawmill that buys our logs. Why?"

"I called him today."

"But the sawmill isn't open on Sundays."

"I tracked down his home number and called him there."

Gus sat down at the second desk, forgetting all about her annoyance over Cash using the one she preferred. Him calling Cal Hayden at home seemed like the tip of an extremely perturbing iceberg, and she was suddenly weak with foreboding.

"And?" she said accusingly when he didn't immediately begin reciting details.

She could get the most forbidding expression on her face he'd ever seen, Cash realized. It dared him to go too far and suggested retribution if he did. For certain, she wasn't sitting there with an open mind.

"Lighten up," he growled. "Cal and I discussed a hell of a good deal today."

"Without consulting me. What deal?" Gus questioned suspiciously.

"He agreed to advance this company money on its standing timber."

Gus's mouth dropped open. "This company does not borrow money!"

"An archaic attitude," Cash said brusquely. "This deal makes good sense. The advance would be repaid as the logs are delivered to the mill. We could buy better equipment and bring our repair costs down to a reasonable figure. Are you aware that this company spent over a hundred thousand dollars on repairs last year? That much unnecessary expense is ludicrous, Gus. It's money that should have been on the profit side of the ledger."

Gus's eyes were dark with fury. "Are *you* aware of the kind of power a loan like that gives a sawmill over a logging company? We've always operated as a free agent, and if one mill doesn't pay enough or short-scales our deliveries, we've been able to haul to another."

"Cal's mill is the closest to the mountain," Cash pointed out. "And according to your own records we've been doing business with his company for over five years."

"But your deal would eliminate our options. It stinks, Cash, and I won't be a party to it." Gus's eyes gleamed. "You can't do it without my approval."

"I knew you'd take that attitude," Cash said coldly, getting up from the desk. "So I put together some figures to prove how wrong you are." With the same sheaf of papers he'd carried outside when Gus had gotten back, he crossed over to the second desk. "Take a look at these." He laid the papers in front of her.

Gus's gaze dropped to the papers, which were laden with neat rows of figures. "In thirty seconds or less?" she said sarcastically.

"Obviously it'll take a while for you to understand what I've done," Cash retorted, just as sarcastically. "But you're not so narrow-minded as to refuse to try, are you?"

Gus wanted to refuse. More than that, she'd like to rip his work into tiny shreds and throw the pieces in his face. Narrow-minded, was she? Archaic? And she hadn't forgotten his other flattering remark about her not being very imaginative in business, either. For one painful second she thought about him calling her his "little ratette" yesterday. He'd lost his sense of humor during the night, apparently, and was treating her today as she'd requested all along, as his business partner—one he didn't have a whole lot of esteem for.

The whole situation was appalling, and maddening. But she could hardly pull a sullen act and refuse to look at his work. Yesterday's big love scene didn't seem real now, as though it had occurred between two other people.

Cash could almost see her wheels turning. If she dug in and refused to even consider the deal, his hands were tied. He wouldn't give up, but a stubborn refusal now would unquestionably hinder the progress he envisioned for the company.

"Gus," he said in a softer tone. "Don't take your anger at me out on the company. This deal would strengthen our financial position, and if you'll give those figures a chance you'll see why. The elements for a profitable operation are already here. All they need is some creative churning."

"Churning," Gus repeated evenly. "Is that what they call debt these days?" She picked up the papers. "I'll look at these, but I despise the idea of debt. It was the way I was raised," she added defensively. "And if my respect for my father's ways offends you, it's something you're going to have to live with. I'm sure you're as much a product of family environment as I am."

Her eyes narrowed suddenly. Why didn't he finance with his own money the equipment that he was so insistent on buying? Why bring in a third party? Any loan would earn interest, and why not collect it himself instead of passing on a sure thing to Cal Hayden?

Cash hated the frost between them, but the alternative to standing firm with Gus was doing everything her way. Still, the words popped out of his mouth before he could stop them. "Where were you last night?"

"With a friend," Gus returned icily. She flushed at the look in Cash's eyes. "*And* her husband. They live on the coast."

Cash visibly relaxed. "Thanks for telling me." He'd had crazy visions all night, from Henry Shanks to a parade of faceless men. Yet he couldn't believe Gus would go from him to another man, no matter how upset she'd been because he'd enticed her into bed. It had been all his doing, Cash knew. Gus would never have made a pass at him. And it wouldn't happen again, even if he had to glue his hands to his sides.

With a closed expression, he walked to a window. "The crew's getting back."

Gus stood up with the sheaf of papers. "Mandy puts out a light supper on Sunday evening," she said to inform him of the routine. She went to the door.

Cash turned. "I'd appreciate hearing your reaction to that work as soon as possible."

"You will," Gus said flatly, and thought, *Believe me, buster, you'll hear it first thing in the morning.*

Seven

Seated on the sofa in the living room so she could see out the front window into the compound, Gus's attention to Cash's work was desultory at best. She began reading with a resentful air and a certainty that it wouldn't amount to a hill of beans. He'd put a bunch of numbers together. So what?

Fifteen minutes later she hadn't looked out the window once. Completely absorbed, she got up, went to the storage room for one of the old calculators, which had once again been relegated to a shelf, toted the heavy machine to the kitchen table along with a pad and pencil and sat down with the papers spread out in front of her.

Cash had done some creative accounting, beginning with last year's actual expenditure for equipment repairs. To that figure he had added the cost of unproductive man hours due to the disabled equipment, and a reasonable estimate of lost log deliveries. There were all sorts of complex computations to arrive at those estimates, but the final cost to the company for broken-down trucks, power saws and the other logging equipment, was a shock to Gus's system. With the calculator, Gus checked Cash's mathematics for herself.

The second part of his report consisted of a projection of profits based on an advance from the sawmill and the purchase of newer equipment. He had allowed a reasonable amount for normal maintenance and a contingency figure for emergency situations, which could occur even with brand-new equipment. Again there were computations of man-hours and log deliveries, pages of them, enough figures to make Gus's head swim. But Cash's final conclusion, an impressive profit despite a sizable interest figure for the use of the sawmill's money, was another shock for Gus.

Was it absolutely accurate? Shuffling papers rather frantically, she started over at page one and fed numbers into the ancient calculator at a furious pace. She filled pages of her pad with her own rows of numbers. At one point, she got up and switched on the kitchen lights, but she was so engrossed in what she was doing at the table, she barely noticed the interruption.

Hours later she sat back, stunned that she could find no flaws in Cash's extremely detailed and imaginative cost studies. He had accurately depicted the company's current financial structure, and proven on paper how beneficial an influx of capital would be, even though borrowed and bearing the current rate of interest.

Gus stared at the disarray of papers, both hers and Cash's, on the table. She would have to admit his thoroughness in the morning, and that she hadn't been able to punch holes in his theories. The thought knotted her stomach, but right was right.

Cash being right on paper didn't reduce Gus's dislike of debt, however. Big Jim had been obsessive about not creating debt, doing without on a regular basis rather than buying on credit. She was the same.

An incident from her marriage arose in Gus's mind. Larry had been eager to buy a new car, which would have meant monthly payments of almost five hundred dollars for several years. No way, she had fervently announced. Their used cars were good enough, and they were paid for. Thinking about it now, Gus wondered if her unrelenting practicality had always been wise.

Maybe it wasn't wise in this instance with Cash, either, but giving the sawmill a legal hold on the company's timber, certainly its most valuable asset, was still a distressing prospect.

A glance at the wall clock surprised Gus. It was nearly midnight. She had long since missed supper while going over numbers for half the night. Rising wearily, she sorted Cash's papers from her own into two stacks.

In the apartment, Cash got up for a drink of water. He'd been sleeping restlessly, awakening at intervals to worry. He stopped at a window to notice lights on in Gus's house, and to wonder if she was up so late because of his work. It was a good sign, if that was the case, indicating a thorough examination of his figures instead of a quick and disinterested glance, which was what he'd been fearing.

He went back to bed feeling hopeful.

Gus groaned when the alarm went off at four-thirty. She groaned again when she heard rain on the roof. Snuggling deeper into the covers, she thought of what she had to do today: Tell Cash his figures had impressed her but she still despised the idea of going into debt. He would have arguments against her attitude, and she would have arguments against *his* arguments. An impasse was in the making, and she wasn't sure she was up to it.

The drizzle on the roof seeped into her thoughts, reminding her of Saturday. Her body began tingling from the memories. Making love with Cash was like something she'd read about in steamy novels. That sort of pleasure could become addictive very quickly. Would a woman compromise principles and ethics to sustain a relationship with a man who gave her such intense pleasure? Why hadn't she found the same thing with some other man? Why with Cash?

It wasn't fair. She hadn't been unhappy before he came along. Ignorance really was bliss, apparently, because she hadn't thought anything was missing from her life. Oh, there'd been moments of envy for friends who seemed to have it all. But certainly she hadn't connected those brief, rare spurts of envy with sex. In fact, sex had been the farthest thing from her mind. Now she wondered if she'd ever think about anything else during her private moments.

Throwing back the covers, Gus jumped out of bed before she could change her mind and decide to stay there for the rest of the rainy day. Mondays were the same on the mountain as anywhere else, the beginning of five days of hard work. After a wake-up shower, she dressed quickly in clean jeans, a cotton shirt and her heavy work boots. Cosmetics were usually ignored during the week, but after brushing her hair she dabbed on a thin layer of lipstick.

The rain was light so Gus carried her waterproof jacket during the walk to the cookhouse. The men's rain jackets were hanging on hooks inside the door, and the crew was already eating when she went in. Cash came in right behind her.

"Morning," he said, looking into her eyes for some clue to her feelings about his work. She looked away so quickly that he detected nothing.

"Good morning." Gus went to the counter and fixed a plate with scrambled eggs and a small piece of ham. With a cup of coffee and the plate, she sat at an empty table. As she'd suspected he would, Cash joined her with his own food.

"Are you going to the woods today?" she questioned.

"I've got some calls to make." Over his cup Cash looked at her. "To equipment dealers. I want some accurate prices."

Gus's mouth tightened. "Don't jump the gun."

"Did you read my report?"

"I read it."

"And?"

Gus took a sip of coffee and set down her cup. "I'd rather discuss it in private. I'm going to the woods but I'll come back as soon as possible. You'll be in the office?"

"I'll be in the office," Cash confirmed. He was going to contact truck and equipment dealers this morning, even though Gus saw gathering price and availability information as "jumping the gun." Accuracy was important to his projections, and he'd tried calling for data yesterday only to learn through message machines that the companies were closed on Sundays.

The men began bringing their dishes to the counter and collecting their jackets and lunch buckets. Gus gulped the rest of her coffee and stood up. "I shouldn't be more than a couple of hours," she said to Cash.

He nodded. "You know where to find me."

When everyone had trooped out of the dining room, Cash sat there wondering if a more profitable future was worth losing Gus over. Not that he'd ever really had Gus. In bed, yes. Once, with no assurances from her of things to come. Rather, with resentment because he'd lured her into something she preferred not being a part of. He couldn't deny that he'd pursued her a whole lot sooner than he should have considering their uneasy alliance in the company.

But she'd hit him hard at their first meeting. He couldn't remember ever being smitten so quickly. Her size and vocation had seemed humorously incompatible. Since, he'd learned how capable she was in the woods. No one could doubt her control of the logging operation, and of the men in the crew. There was a question in Cash's mind if he would ever attain Gus's expertise in that area of the company.

His personal feelings for Gus were still present in the core of his system, but surrounding them in a strange, unpleasant way was a sense of emptiness. A void. He'd be wise to maintain it. Maybe not contented, but wise.

Just then Mandy came in. "Oh, you're still here. I thought everyone had gone."

Cash got to his feet. "I'm going, too."

"Don't let me chase you off." Mandy began loading dirty dishes from the counter onto a tray and commented, "Nasty day out there."

The gray day fit Cash's mood. "Yes, it is."

"How's that pup doing?" Mandy asked as Cash headed for the door.

Cash stopped to smile. "Doodles is doing fine. He's good company."

Mandy sent him a look of understanding. "It can get lonely so far from town. I like it, though."

"I like it, too, Mandy, but you're right. It can get lonely."

He stepped out into the drizzle. Indeed, the mountain could be lonely. Especially during the weekend when everyone else scattered to friends and family. Ignoring the soft rainfall, Cash took his time crossing the compound to the office. How were his brothers faring in Montana and Nevada? He could call them and find out.

Just the thought of contact with his family made Cash feel better, and he picked up his pace and took the stairs to the porch of the office in one bound.

Gus got back around ten-thirty. Despite her rain gear, she felt damp clear through. The rain wasn't hard enough to shut down the job, but it wasn't pleasant working with moisture seeping into every possible gap in clothing. Everyone treated their boots with a waterproofing compound, which saved them from wet feet, but it wasn't possible to completely lock out a constant, long-lasting drizzle.

After detouring to her house to get the two stacks of papers from the kitchen table, Gus went to the office, took off her jacket and hard hat and hung them on hooks. Cash was on the phone and using the second desk, which gave her a pang of guilt. Ignoring it, she went to the desk by the window and sat down.

"Thanks for the information," he said into the phone. "I'll be in touch." After putting down the phone he looked at Gus and repeated Mandy's comment on the weather. "Nasty day out there."

"We get a lot of rain, so we're used to it." Gus tapped the papers in front of her. "Are you busy, or are you ready to talk about this?"

"I'm ready." The latent tension in Cash's system intensified. Gus's reaction to his work was crucial. He wasn't going to be stopped, but a negative attitude would slow him down. Particularly if she was still dead-set against change regardless if its logic.

Gus took a breath. "Your work is—" she paused to find the precise word "—impressive." Cash's hopes immediately tripled. "It took me awhile to understand what you did," Gus continued. "And I don't mind admitting that I checked the mathematics of your computations. The bottom line, Cash, is that I couldn't find any theoretical or mathematical errors. In other words, I can't disagree with anything in these papers."

Cash didn't know whether to jump up and shout or give in to the sudden weakening relief he felt.

"At the same time," Gus went on, "I can't see that this work changes anything." Across the space between the two desks, Gus sent him a direct look. "The thought of giving anyone a legal hold on our timber is disturbing. The timber is the backbone of this company. Without it—"

"But you're looking at my proposal with an open mind," Cash interjected eagerly. "Gus, that's all I ask."

"No, it isn't," she rebutted evenly. "Now you're going to try to talk me into agreeing with your point of view."

Cash got up and walked to a window. Gus was right. Reading and understanding his work wasn't enough. Even agreeing with his theories and conclusions wasn't enough. There had to be some way to bring them closer together in outlook. Damn, if they ever really agreed, the sky would be the limit for this company.

He turned around. "I appreciate the time you put in on this, Gus. Truthfully I didn't expect complete accord on my figures, so I'm darned appreciative of that, as well. But we can't just drop it at that. There has to be a way to make it work without compromising your principles."

Gus stared, surprised that he hadn't immediately launched into a campaign to convince her of the narrow-mindedness of her attitude. "I...suppose we could talk about it," she said slowly.

She had just made a tremendous concession, Cash realized, and his hopes soared again. All through the night he'd only half-slept, awakening again and again to worry about this very discussion. What would Gus say? What would he say? The worst scenario would have been her flat-out refusal to talk at all; the best would have been total agreement. The second best had just happened.

He returned to his desk, geared for conversation. "Your primary objection is centered on giving Cal Hayden a hold on our timber."

"Aside from my dislike of debt of any kind, yes."

"Gus, the only way to give this company a jump-start is to take on some debt. I've got a list here." Cash held up a piece of paper. "I talked to a dozen different equipment companies this morning and compiled prices and availability. I'm not thinking of brand-new anything, other than power saws. But every truck we've got is unreliable."

She didn't agree or disagree. Needing newer and better equipment wasn't the issue; how they procured it was. "You're talking about a huge sum of money," she pointed out.

"The final figure is less than I put into that proposal. The equipment companies are hungry, Gus. They're loaded with good used trucks because of the recession, and because of the problems between environmentalists and the U.S. Forest Service, which have slowed down the logging industry." Cash leaned forward. "Our timber is almost unbelievably valuable right now, Gus. Now's the time to—"

She interrupted curtly. "But its value wouldn't be ours anymore if we signed it over to Hayden."

"He would control it only to the extent of the loan."

"I don't want Cal Hayden calling the shots," Gus said sharply. "The value of our timber far surpasses the amount of the loan cited in your proposal. Subordinating every stick on this mountain for one influx of cash isn't smart!" She got up suddenly and hurried over to one of the file cabinets to pull open a drawer. Coming out with a thick folder, she left the drawer hanging open and walked to Cash's desk to lay down the folder. "I'm sure you've already seen this, but take another look at it."

Cash opened the folder and nodded. "I've seen it. It's your father's layout of the mountain." Big Jim had mapped the mountain within a numbered grid, designating logging sites within each grid to keep close track of the various areas and stages of timber growth. Cash had been impressed when he'd first studied the work, and he knew Gus faithfully lived by it, moving the logging operation periodically in conjunction with Big Jim's long-term plan.

He raised his eyes to Gus. "What are you thinking?"

Gus placed one hand on Cash's desk and leaned over it to point at the folder. "There's more than enough timber in any one of those grids to back the amount of the loan in your proposal."

Cash looked down at the mapped grid. Within seconds a grin broke out on his face. "Gus, you're absolutely brilliant!"

She backed up two full steps. "What did I say?" The words were no sooner out of her mouth when she understood what was going through his mind. The grid, of course, and its relationship to the loan. Cash's eyes were an excited bright blue and boring into hers with a startling intensity. Uneasily she watched him reach for the phone and punch out a number.

"Can you go with me to talk to Cal Hayden?" he asked her while waiting for someone to pick up on the other end. "Hello," he said into the phone before Gus could answer. "Cal Hayden, please. This is Cash Saxon." He put his hand over the mouthpiece. "Will you go to see Hayden with me, Gus?"

Second thoughts were flitting through Gus's mind. It might be a brilliant idea to talk Cal Hayden into tying the loan to only one particular grid of timber, thereby leaving the balance of the mountain unencumbered, but had she actually agreed to pursue the deal?

Frowning, she turned away, shaken by the possibility of Cash railroading her. Had that "grid" idea been hers at all, or merely his clever method of gaining her cooperation? Certainly a bullheaded I'm-right-and-you're-wrong approach wouldn't have worked. Neither would self-righteous anger. But drawing her into the scenario and naming her brilliant at her first positive remark had dragged her across the line and into his territory so fast, there'd been no time to say yea or nay.

Listening to Cash arranging an appointment for that afternoon, Gus went to a window and stared out. The second he put down the phone, she turned around with a warning. "I didn't agree to anything."

"I know you didn't. But tying only one grid of timber to the loan was your idea, all the same. And it's a skillful, intelligent approach to our situation." Cash was looking at her with new respect. He knew he'd been prepared to put up all the timber on the mountain as collateral, undoubtedly jumping into the deal a little too hastily. In this case Gus's reluctance had forced him to slow down, obviously the best course. Cash vowed to remember this unexpected lesson in the future.

"Gus, I really would like you to go with me. Whatever we ultimately decide, Hayden should see a united front."

For some reason Gus again thought about Cash's own wealth. Why would he pay someone else interest when he could earn it himself? He could link the loan to the timber to assure repayment if he had any doubts about getting his money back. It just didn't make sense to Gus. If she had any personal money lying around, she wouldn't hesitate to loan it to the company for a second.

Regardless, there were some subjects too touchy to spring on a person, even on a completely incomprehensible partner.

But she should attend the meeting with Cal Hayden to protect her own interests, if nothing else. "Fine," she said distantly. "I'll go along. Did I hear you say three this afternoon?"

"Three it is. What time should we leave here?"

"Around two." Gus took her jacket and hard hat from the wall hooks. "I'll be back in plenty of time."

Cash followed her to the door. "Are you going back to the woods?"

Gus fit the yellow hard hat onto her head. "Yes. It's been raining harder and I want to check on the mud."

"What about the mud?"

"When the mud gets too deep, I shut down the job." Gus glanced at Cash's cowboy boots. "Still didn't buy those logging boots?"

Cash cleared his throat. "Not yet."

"Maybe today," Gus drawled with some sarcasm. "The sawmill's about twenty miles on the other side of Hamilton. We could stop and shop. Then maybe *you* can check on the mud the next time it rains."

"I can do it this time," Cash snapped. What in hell had made him think Gus had softened just because she'd spoken civilly for a few minutes? "You don't think I'm doing my share, do you? Come back inside and *I'll* drive out to the damned job!"

Gus dismissed his demand with an arrogant wave of her hand. Descending the stairs to the ground she called over her shoulder, "Don't strain yourself, Saxon." In the next breath she felt petty and about two-inches high. Even if Cash had originally come up with the idea to go out to the woods and check the density of mud the men were battling, she wouldn't have trusted his judgment. Her anger wasn't because of duty in the rain, but because he'd maneuvered her into talking to Cal Hayden. Just as he'd maneuvered her into his bed the other day.

Cash grabbed his jacket and hard hat and raced from the office. Gus's pickup was started and beginning to move when he yanked open the passenger door. She slammed on the brakes. "What're you trying to do, get yourself killed?" she yelled angrily.

Plopping onto the seat, Cash slammed the door shut. "What I'm trying to do is find your best side," he snarled. "That's supposing you have one. I'm beginning to see that hope as a pipe dream."

"I'm just positive you're lying awake nights worrying about my best side," Gus drawled. "Don't waste your breath or my time in half-truths, okay? All you're worried about is putting this company in such deep muck, it will never get out. And I'd like to know why. With your background and money, why in hell are you here making my life miserable over a loan you don't need?"

"You think you know everything there is to know about me, don't you?"

Gus was driving on automatic pilot, skirting water-filled potholes and staying on the familiar road by pure instinct. "I know nothing about you!" she shouted. "How could I?"

"If you're so totally in the dark, why are you making judgments about my motives?" Cash shouted back. "I'm broke, dammit! My whole family is broke!"

They both fell into a stunned silence. Gus took her eyes from the muddy road to shoot him a glance. Cash sat as though frozen in place, his mouth a thin, grim line. Several miles later, Gus spoke. "Why didn't you tell me that right away?"

"Would it have made a difference?"

"I don't know." At least some of Cash's perplexing behavior was making sense now. "It might have." Gus stole another glance at his stony profile and groaned inwardly. Talk about the male ego. His had just been delivered a lethal blow—granted, by his own words—and now he couldn't even bring himself to look at her.

"I hope you don't think your personal financial situation means anything to me," she said matter-of-factly. "Most of my friends are broke, or at best living from payday to payday. That's the norm, Cash. That's the way ninety-nine percent of the population lives."

He smirked. "Where'd you get that statistic?"

"God, the smugness of the wealthy," Gus said with exaggerated sarcasm. When she received a sharp glance for the remark, she added, "I suspect you were part of the one percent minority for most of your life, so save your disgust for someone it will impress. And for pete's sake, don't be embarrassed!"

Cash turned narrowed eyes on her. "My only embarrassment is caused by the way I told you, not by the information itself. I didn't come here mourning the loss of the family fortune. This company was exciting to me. I was eager to meet Big Jim Parrish and just as eager to get started in the logging business."

Gus listened silently, unable to doubt the sincerity behind Cash's outburst. He wasn't finished. "Instead of a man by the name of Big Jim, I met a five-foot-tall woman who claimed to be running the show. You might not find that incongruous but it struck me that way. A lady logger? Yeah, it struck me as just a tad out of the ordinary.

"On top of that, she made her distaste very clear. How dare a Saxon intrude after so many years? How dare he come up with any ideas different than her own?"

"Just a minute," Gus interjected sharply. "The routines of this company were set long ago, and not by me and not by a Saxon. You bet you intruded. Don't expect an apology because I was surprised when you came knocking on my door."

"Expect an apology? From you? Gus, have you ever once admitted you might be wrong about anything? Well, let me tell you something, lady. You're dead wrong about the future of this company. It's stagnating, barely surviving, and one of these days the result of your stubborn refusal to see what's really happening is going to bring the whole thing tumbling down around your ears. Right now you're holding the operation together with guts, spit and hope. And a damned good mechanic," Cash added wryly. "Without Lloyd on the job seven days a week, this place would fall apart."

"I understand Lloyd's value as well as you do," Gus retorted.

"Do you also understand that his earnings last year were more than what the partnership netted? The partners should make at least as much money as the hired help!"

Gus was glad to see the logging site. She was tired of bickering. But Cash's arguments had dug into her psyche all the same. Of course the partners should make as much money as the hired help. And, yes, relying on old, worn-out equipment was eventually going to catch up with them all.

She parked the pickup thinking that Cash had won. The thought of telling him so raised the fine hairs on the back of her neck, but she had no choice. She turned in the seat.

"You're right and I'm wrong. Is that what you want to hear?" she said angrily.

Cash looked at her. "Do you have to put it so crassly? Gus, it's not a matter of who's right. It's a matter of getting the company on the right track. That's all I'm trying to do. You're crucial to the operation. Don't you think I know that? To attain any lasting success, we have to work together. Tearing at each other like this over every decision is stupid and destructive."

His voice gentled. Gus was more than a business partner, and he hated fighting with her. "Let's be friends, Gussie. Let's work together and make this company into the best it can be."

She swallowed the sudden lump in her throat, but it was impossible to completely dissolve her resentment. "I can't guarantee friendship," she said unsteadily.

"How about if we don't look for guarantees and merely try?"

After a hesitation, Gus nodded her head. "Agreed." Her gaze was on the dreary, waterlogged landscape. "I'm going to shut down the job for the rest of the day." She looked at Cash, as though anticipating discord. "Do you disagree?"

"I'll never second-guess any decision you make in the woods," he said quietly. "This is your domain, Gus. Maybe mine's in the office. I'm not sure of my role in the operation yet. I'm still a novice out here and maybe I always will be, though God knows I want to learn."

It was as though Gus was suddenly standing in his shoes, in his admittedly uncomfortable cowboy boots. She knew now why he hadn't bought those two hundred dollar logging boots, and why he was driving a used Wagoneer, and why he'd gone to someone else for a loan to upgrade the company equipment.

Maybe she even understood why he'd brought Doodles to camp. Cash was alone out here, without family, without friends, and a puppy was a lot better than nothing. She'd been a witch to him, defying his every word and attempt to get involved. The only place he'd reached her was in bed, and judging from his attitude ever since, even he knew a sexual relationship had no place in this partnership.

The realization didn't make Gus particularly happy. Thinking about the laughter in Cash's eyes until she'd gone off and left him to worry all night, she wondered if her hasty and inconsiderate departure hadn't destroyed the best thing they'd had going for them.

Sighing, Gus forced herself to look at him. Cash's eyes met hers. Neither spoke, but the war between them seemed to be over.

After a minute Gus reached for the door handle. "I'll go tell the men to wrap it up for the day. Please stay here. There's no point in your getting your feet soaked. I won't be long."

Cash did as she asked, maybe because she'd said please, maybe because, as he'd told her, this was her domain.

Now all he had to do was tie down and stabilize his own.

Eight

Cash drove his Wagoneer to the meeting with Cal Hayden and Gus rode along. They were both unusually subdued and spoke very little. Gus had changed from her work clothes into tan slacks, an off-white cotton sweater and high-heeled boots. She had put on makeup and a dab of cologne, not to entice Cash or to draw Hayden's notice but because her own spirits had needed a lift.

Things were happening too fast for Gus, who would rather ponder any change in routine for a good long while before gradually sliding into it. One factor seemed positive: she understood Cash better now. His motivation for rushing the company headlong into debt was his own need of income. Still, why should his driving ambition have to be her ambition?

The most persistent question remaining in Gus's mind after Cash's startling information about the demise of his family's fortune, was why he had made such blatant passes at her. He really didn't seem like a man who chased every woman he ran across, and yet what else could she think?

Her own participation could be blamed on her nonexistent love life, and on the fact that the only love life she ever did have had been about as exciting as tap water. Cash had been exciting. More accurately, Cash *was* exciting. Riding beside him as he drove the familiar roads to Hamilton and then beyond, Gus couldn't deny that he affected her.

That private piece of knowledge perplexed Gus. Why did she have so little control over her own responses, particularly when caused by a man who had apparently lost interest? At moments she felt embarrassment because she'd been so easy, at other times anger whipped through her because Cash could obviously turn his emotions on and off like a light switch and she couldn't.

They were not at all alike. Their personalities, in fact, were so far apart it would be a miracle if the two of them ever got along. Was this to be her future? Uneasy truces? One of them constantly pushing the other one into decisions about the company?

"Is that the turn?" Cash questioned.

Gus aligned her thoughts with the road. The sawmill was situated about a half mile off the highway. There were signs indicating the Spring Valley Lumber Company, so there'd been no reason whatsoever for him to ask about the turn.

"That's it," she said coolly.

After taking the turn, Cash pulled the Wagoneer over to the side of the road and put the shifting lever in Park. He looked at Gus. "Are you okay?"

"I'm fine. Why did you stop?"

"You've been awfully quiet. Gus, we're doing the right thing."

"I'm here, aren't I?"

"But you're not happy about it."

Gus was staring straight ahead. "You've worn me down and I'm here. Don't expect elation over it." She was trying very hard to look at this whole thing logically. As much as she loathed the idea of debt, Cash wasn't wrong about the company needing money. The equipment was bound to give out permanently one of these days, so debt could only be avoided for so long. Fine. She'd come to grips with that fact.

But losing the argument to the man who had taken her to the stars in his bed was a personal affront that kept digging at her. What's more, it wasn't something she could explain or even hint at.

Studying her stubbornly set profile, Cash wished he could take her in his arms and eradicate the dissension between them. If it were only that easy, he thought with an inward sigh as he moved the shifting lever back into Drive. Making love with Gus had only complicated their already complicated relationship. His decision to avoid any more such intimacy was only prudent and he would abide by it, difficult as it was.

Cal Hayden was waiting for them, smiling all over the place. Gus had met with Cal before, so the man wasn't a stranger. But today he was a whole lot friendlier than usual, she noticed, obviously just thrilled to death to get this deal on-line.

Cash was the real surprise. His confidence while shaking Cal's hand and putting them on the right footing was amazing. Maybe no one was a stranger to Cash Saxon, Gus mused, but somewhere in his background he'd picked up the enviable trait of total composure while meeting a new and important business acquaintance.

They sat in Cal's office, which Gus had seen a few times before. It was an unpretentious room, with wood-paneled walls and rather colorless, commercial-grade carpeting. The furniture was heavy and bore the scars of many years of usage.

Cal beamed across his big desk. "Well, I talked to the owners and they agreed to advancing the money you need."

"We appreciate your quick action, Cal," Cash said with a glance at Gus. "Gus, suppose you tell Cal what you and I discussed this morning."

For a second Gus didn't know if Cash was putting her on the hot seat or merely presenting that "united front" he'd mentioned. Certainly his request was drawing her into the conversation.

"All right," she said evenly. "Mr. Hayden, as you probably know, our company has always logged selectively. You've seen Dad's map of the mountain, I'm sure."

"Big Jim gave me a copy of it years ago," Cal concurred.

"I thought that might be the case. Each grid of the map contains a specific amount of standing timber, which is growth-documented on an annual basis. Your copy of Dad's work has to be very outdated without the annual updates. But my point is that we know quite accurately how much timber is in each grid, and when it will be ripe for harvesting again."

"Go on," Cal prompted when Gus paused. The truth was, she wasn't sure she should be the one doing the talking right now. Wasn't this Cash's baby? Certainly she hadn't contacted Cal Hayden for a loan. "Cash will take it from here," she said quietly.

"Gus brought this to my attention this morning, Cal," Cash said calmly. "Any one of the grids on Big Jim's map contains more than enough timber to collateralize the advance you and I discussed."

Cal frowned. "That's probably true, but collateralizing the loan wasn't my only intent, Cash. It's no secret that private timber is at a premium right now. I'd like to see—and I know the owners feel the same—a strong bond between your company and ours."

"A long-term contract?" Gus interjected with a sharp edge on her voice.

Cal grinned. "If I can get you to sign one, yes. Your father never would, which I'm sure you know."

"Is the loan contingent on a contract?" Gus questioned.

Cal looked at Cash. "How do you feel about a contract, Cash?"

Cash thought for a moment before answering. "Maybe I have to ask the same question that Gus just did. Is the loan contingent on she and I signing a long-term contract?"

A silence stretched while Cal gave it some thought. "I take it you're suggesting the loan be collateralized by only a portion of your timber?"

"By one grid," Gus replied. At Cal Hayden's suddenly raised eyebrow, she added, "You can pick which one."

"I think we're talking about guarantees here," Cal said reflectively. "This mill needs your timber, Gus. Attempting to keep you in the dark on that point would only be counterproductive to this conversation. The owners suggested frankness, and I agree. I think you're well aware of the contribution the Spring Valley Lumber Company makes to the economy of the area. Forest Service timber sales have all but dried up. Without a good source of private timber this mill could very well run into some serious problems, and in the not too distant future.

"When Cash called to discuss an advance to modernize your equipment, I immediately saw an opportunity to align our companies in a mutually beneficial way. We need your timber, you need our cash. It could be one heck of a good deal for both of us."

"We only need one loan," Gus said with a pleading glance at Cash.

But Cash didn't see the plea. He was thinking, getting a glimpse of a much larger picture than he'd arrived here with. Working in conjunction with a sawmill that was admittedly long on cash and short on timber could indeed be beneficial.

"We log on our schedule," he said to Cal.

"Of course," Cal agreed. "That's completely understood up-front."

"One loan, one grid," Cash said. "An agreement on the price of delivered logs based on current market rates, and an escape clause should either of us be dissatisfied."

"Agreed," Cal said.

Gus's startled gaze darted from man to man. "No long-term contract," Cash said. "But a simple agreement naming the Spring Valley Lumber Company as the primary purchaser of our timber shouldn't be a problem."

"Agreed," Cal repeated after a moment of thought. "That's been the arrangement for five years now even without something down on paper. The owners would prefer a binding contract, but I think they would accept the sort of agreement you're suggesting.''

"We won't borrow any money we don't need," Cash said. "But should the need arise, the sawmill will make the advance using whichever grid we're logging at the time as collateral. The loan would be repaid as the logs from that particular grid are delivered.''

"Agreed," Cal exclaimed.

This was going way over Gus's head. "Just a minute," she said sharply. "We're here to discuss only one loan. Cash, you're talking as though we're going to need additional loans every few months.''

"Not at all," Cash replied. "Hopefully we will never need to borrow money again." The angry, stubborn glint in Gus's eyes wasn't appeased by that assurance. He knew she thought in terms of the precise present. Today they needed a specific amount of money, which should be the extent of this discussion. What he and Cal both grasped and Gus apparently didn't were the advantages of a long-term agreement.

Still, he had discovered only this morning the good sense of scrutinizing a business deal from every angle. Without Gus's adamant objections to giving the mill a hold on all of the Parrish-Saxon timber for one modest loan, he might have made that dire blunder. Her input on this much broader plan could be very important.

Cash's gaze returned to Cal. "I think that about covers it for now, Cal. Gus and I will go over what we discussed, and one of us will get back to you tomorrow.''

Everyone stood up and shook hands. "I can have the paperwork and the check prepared within a day or two," Cal told them. "You could have your money by Thursday at the latest.''

Gus was almost rigid as they left, wondering if she was justifiably furious or merely dense. Certainly she saw Hayden's and Cash's discussion as something alien and vastly different than what she'd expected.

She was silent until they were seated in the Wagoneer and leaving the grounds of the sawmill. Then she cast Cash a murderous look and asked, "What in hell was that all about?"

"It's very simple, merely a means to—"

"Don't patronize me! It *wasn't* simple. It was miles from what we went there to talk about. You know my views on the company remaining an independent operation. You know—"

"Stop yelling, dammit! Gus, you fly off the handle too fast. The only thing Hayden is getting out of the deal is an agreement to give him first crack at our logs. You've been doing that anyway."

"Not in writing."

"Putting it in writing is no more than a courteous formality. With escape clauses in the document, either him or us could cancel it anytime we wish."

"It didn't sound like that to me," Gus said, fuming.

"He's willing to do almost anything to ensure his mill of a steady supply of timber. And can you blame him? What good is a sawmill without logs? You heard what he said about his company's unstable future. Cal was being deadly honest with us, Gus. The man is not out to undercut us in some shady deal."

Gus was calming down and regretting her outburst. What Cash had said about her flying off the handle too fast was the painful truth. But she'd never had an iota of trouble with her temper before Cash's appearance on the mountain, which in itself raised her dander.

"I never accused Cal Hayden of dishonesty," she said in a less strident tone. "But the deal you two were tossing around will tie us to the Spring Valley Lumber Company."

"To our benefit, as well as theirs," Cash replied.

"What happens if we want to sell our logs to another mill?"

"The only logs we'll be legally obligated to sell to Spring Valley are those pledged as loan collateral."

Gus's eyes flashed again. "Then why make an agreement naming them as our primary purchaser?"

"It will give the sawmill owners a modicum of security."

"You're thinking about future loans," Gus accused darkly.

"What I'm thinking about is the future in general." They were approaching the outskirts of Hamilton, and Cash slowed the Wagoneer to the posted speed limit. "Gus, right now we're thinking in terms of one relatively small loan, with no plans in mind for further expansion. But why not keep the door open for any contingency? This deal with Hayden assures our company of a financially untroubled future."

"Your definition of debt and mine are worlds apart," Gus said with some bitterness. "You're talking me into seeing your side again, and I don't like it."

"Everything is divided into sides with you," Cash said with a discouraged sigh. "And maybe I don't like that. For certain I don't like our constant bickering."

"And you think I do?" Gus turned her head to glare at him.

"Maybe we should do something about it," Cash said. "It just occurred to me that one of us could buy the other out."

The suggestion shocked Gus into silence. Buy him out? With what, a loan from Cal Hayden? That would put her into the soup for sure. As for him buying her out, forget it!

"I will *never* sell my father's business," she said with unmistakable passion. "And I won't borrow money to buy you out!"

Cash nodded grimly. "That's just about what I thought you'd say. All right, fine, we're both stuck. So how about a little cooperation? I'm not saying we should agree on every single aspect of the operation, but we should be able to discuss opposing viewpoints without anger."

The shock of his buy or sell suggestion was still careening through Gus's system. It was one idea that had bypassed her completely. If she had the money right now she could be rid of Cash Saxon for all time. How much would it take?

The thought was surprisingly discomfiting. Instead of elation from picturing herself in sole operation again, Gus felt a most peculiar emptiness. Confusion set in, and her shoulders slumped.

"Do what you want," she said in a near whisper.

"Pardon?"

"Do what you want with the company. You'll do it anyway, with or without my sanction. And maybe you're right. God help us both, I hope you are."

Cash wheeled the Wagoneer to a parking space at the curb. They were in the middle of town with cars driving by and pedestrians on the sidewalk. Cash turned and laid his right arm along the top of the seat. "Don't sound so beaten," he said softly. "Gus, we both want the same thing, a long and successful life for the company. But we think differently. You're extremely conservative and I'm... Well, believe it or not, I didn't know what I was until recently. Did you ever hear the old saying, 'If you snooze, you lose'? Gus, I snoozed my whole life. I'm not snoozing now. I feel alive. I feel excited. There's a reason to get up in the morning, and something with substance to do every hour of the day."

Slowly Gus's face turned his way. "You like taking chances."

"I don't know if 'like' is the right word, but taking a chance is sometimes necessary." They were looking directly into each other's eyes, and Cash's thoughts abruptly deserted the company and landed on Gus. He'd taken a very big chance with her, probably prematurely, but why shouldn't they be more than business partners? His feelings for Gus weren't clearly defined beyond sexual desire, but they were much too strong to ignore indefinitely.

Cash touched her hair with his fingertips and saw the sudden knowledge in her eyes that the mood in the Wagoneer had just changed. She ducked her head to elude the contact. "Please don't."

Cash drew his hand back, but moved closer to her. "Gus, you and I have more than one problem to solve. There's getting along within the company, and then there's...getting along in private."

His voice had dropped to a sexy pitch, and she was becoming very uneasy. "We're parked on the main street of town, in case you haven't noticed. Please...let's just go home."

"That word has a nice sound, don't you think? Home." Cash pronounced the word as though enjoying its flavor. "Gus, that's what I want to do here, make a home. Is that so terrible? I never meant to disrupt your life."

"You've got me so confused I don't know which way is up," Gus whispered.

"I know." Cash let his hand drift back to her hair, and this time she didn't duck away from his touch. "But it doesn't have to be that way, honey. I hate fighting with you. Hell, I hate fighting with anyone. That's something else I just recently learned about myself. This whole venture has been a learning process for me, Gus."

He gently brushed strands of her hair back from her temple. A shiver went up Gus's spine. No matter how bitter their arguments or how far apart their attitudes, there was something mysterious and powerful between them, something that could ignite and flame very quickly.

But the thrills in Gus's body alarmed her, and she pulled away again.

"You still don't trust me, do you?" Cash questioned.

"I think you're capable of turning on the charm when it suits your purpose," Gus replied in an unsteady voice.

"My attraction to you isn't even remotely related to the company," Cash rebutted. "And I don't 'turn on' the charm, Gus. Everything personal between us has happened naturally, merely because you're a beautiful woman and I can't help noticing. Touching you isn't a devious plot to undermine your position in the company. Do you think I could do what you do in the woods? I admire your knowledge, Gus, and maneuvering you out of the company would be the stupidest move I could make."

Gus was inhaling his scent, and feeling his nearness seeping into her own system. Karen had suggested she was falling for Cash, and the thought was suddenly uppermost in Gus's mind. It wasn't like her to respond to a man this way, regardless of good looks and charm. She responded like crazy to Cash, and it had to mean something. Dear God, was she falling in love?

Gus turned her head to look at Cash with a new fear behind her probing gaze. The unusual expression Cash saw on her face made his pulse go wild, and he clasped the back of her head. She gasped. "What are you do—?"

His mouth on hers smothered the rest of her startled question. Instantly, from her outraged sputtering and wriggling away from him, he realized he'd misinterpreted that inquiring look. "Hey...I'm sorry," he said quickly. "I thought..."

"Every time you get an idea, I end up in trouble," Gus snapped. "Give us both a break and *stop* thinking, okay!"

"Don't get mad again," Cash pleaded. "We were making some real headway."

"If I give an inch, you take a mile," Gus accused. "Even if I were inclined to forget business and...and fool around with you again, I wouldn't do it in broad daylight in the middle of Hamilton!"

Cash moved over, then merely sat there staring broodingly out the windshield. Gus sent him a sharp glance. "Will you please get this rig moving?"

"Sure, why not?" Cash said flatly. The Wagoneer was back on the street and moving with traffic in the blink of an eye.

Gus sat ramrod straight. They were several miles out of town before either spoke. "Sorry I offended you," Cash said in a voice as distant as the stars. "It won't happen again."

His wounded ego coming on top of Gus's newfound worry of falling in love seemed like a final straw to her. "You've got the company in the palm of your hand, Cash. Don't expect to find me there as well."

"You're a hard woman, Gus."

"I'm hard?" Gus's voice cracked. "What do you think you are?"

"A nice guy," Cash instantly retorted. "Which you'd discover for yourself if you'd ever let yourself get past the mental and emotional blocks you threw up at first sight of me. You and I could have it all, a good business and... Hell, forget it. I wouldn't touch you again if you begged me."

Gus's mouth dropped open. Did he have to win *every* argument? Where did he get his zingers?

She'd been confused enough before; now she could barely think. Tears began building behind her eyes, burning her nose, and she turned her face to the side window to blink furiously out of his range of vision.

How could she even consider the concept of falling in love with him? Was she crazy?

By the time they were on the final stretch of mountain road just before reaching the camp, Gus had conquered her urge to cry and she had also regained some of her normal spunk. Maybe she'd damaged his ego with her refusal to kiss him, but her own ego took a battering every time they were together.

"Just so you know," she said in a clear, steady voice. "You won't have to stay alert to the possibility of my begging you for anything, least of all a touch."

"Cut it out, Gus," Cash growled. "I keep promising myself to keep my distance and then, too damned often, I turn around and rationalize the decision into something else. I can't help being attracted to you, and every so often I even get the crazy idea that what I'm feeling is more than raging hormones. Like I said, we're both stuck. Let's try to make the best of a lousy situation, okay?"

So now it was a "lousy situation." Well, maybe that term summed it up as well as any. But what were those feelings he'd referred to? Did he mean he felt something for her beyond an occasional yen to take her to bed?

Gus stewed about it for the remainder of the silent drive. Was it possible he was noticing peculiar, questionable feelings for her, as she was with him? Didn't either of them have any control over their emotions? Surely love couldn't bloom in this infertile setting. She cast him a furtive glance and saw the unyielding set of his jaw, a habit he'd picked up in the short time he'd been here. Had she caused it? He'd arrived with laughter seasoning his words and facial expressions, and now he didn't laugh at all.

A loss she couldn't quite grasp ached in the pit of her stomach. What had she gained from bucking Cash's infiltration of the company? Why had she panicked in the first place? Yes, a Saxon materializing without a dram of warning had been a shock. But she'd always known the company was a partnership. Financial statements and modest divisions of profit had always been sent east; she had put reports and a few small checks in the mail herself.

The second the Wagoneer stopped in the compound, Gus opened the door to get out.

"Just a minute." Cash turned off the engine. "What're we going to tell Cal in the morning? Are we in or out?"

Admitting her own petulant, selfish behavior was a blow for Gus. An apology took shape in her mind, but it seemed so inadequate. Besides, in her present state of emotional distress, she wasn't sure she could start baring her soul without going too far.

Her eyes darted to Cash's and then quickly away. "I vote yes."

Startled, Cash sat there and watched her jump out and hurry off in the direction of her house. His eyes narrowed reflectively. Her affirmative vote had been unexpected, particularly since it hadn't been accompanied by argumentative cautions and ultimatums.

In the next heartbeat he realized his attention had focused on the swaying motion of her little behind in those tan slacks. He disgustedly slapped the steering wheel, wondering why he kept thinking of intimacy with a woman who wanted no part of him. When exactly had he turned into such a damned fool?

Nine

With the loan from the Spring Valley Lumber Company increasing the Parrish-Saxon Company bank account, Cash began making preparations to tour the truck and equipment outlets that he'd telephoned.

"When will you be free to go?" he asked Gus on Saturday morning.

They were in the office, with Gus seated at the desk near the window and Cash too excited to sit at all. She had been trying to concentrate on some paperwork and was well aware of Cash's nervous pacing.

She looked up. "I'm not going with you, Cash." Before the alarm on his face could reach his voice, she calmly added, "You could be gone for a week, and it's only sensible for one of us to stay here and keep the operation on-line. I think you should take Lloyd. He understands machinery better than you and I put together. His advice, especially with trucks, would be invaluable."

Cash had thought of that very concept, but had been hesitant to suggest that Gus stay behind. This wasn't a pleasure trip, but it felt like one to him. Not that the trucks would be off-the-showroom-floor new. He'd be looking for good used merchandise and keeping his eyes peeled for bargains.

Sensible or not, Gus's generous attitude was surprising. "Are you sure?" he questioned.

"I'm sure," Gus replied. "Take Lloyd."

Cash paced another circle. "I could call you before buying anything major."

"I'd appreciate that, thank you."

"Our old trucks aren't worth a whole lot, but they'll have some trade-in value."

"They should have."

"The dealers might want to come out here and take a look at them."

Gus laid down her pencil. "If they do and you're still gone, I can show them around."

This new politeness of Gus's had Cash stymied. Since the day they'd gone to talk to Cal, Gus had been speaking to him without anger or resentment. He liked it but he didn't understand her almost miraculous turnabout.

Shoving his hands into the back pockets of his jeans, Cash teetered on the heels of his boots to give her a speculative look. "Uh . . . I don't want to do anything to change what's going on, but did something happen I'm not aware of?"

Gus had wondered if he would have the nerve to come right out and ask about her more cooperative attitude. She'd seen puzzled expressions on his face quite a few times during the past few days, and knew he was questioning her better mood.

But she was still working on sorting out all of the disturbing factors of this relationship and was still a long way from conclusions.

"Let's just say that I'm finally coming to terms with inevitability," she said quietly. That much was true. One could battle inevitability for only so long. Cash was a visible and vocal part of the company now. Fighting that apparently irrevocable fact was only spinning her wheels.

As for the personal aspect of their troubling relationship, Gus had been trying to draw her thoughts away from the word *love*. Chemistry did not constitute love. Cash mentioning incomprehensible feelings did not constitute love. Karen suggesting that Gus might be falling for her partner did not constitute love. Logically there was no reason for her to be thinking about love at all.

And yet the perturbing word was keeping her awake nights, and the memory of their rainy Saturday afternoon together just kept getting more intense. At times she could hardly look at Cash. Visualizing him naked during mundane conversations was embarrassing and physically disturbing. There were stressful moments when she wondered if her own previously all but ignored libido wasn't playing tricks on her by magnifying an ordinary experience into something magical. Had their lovemaking really been as powerful as she remembered?

However specific and painful her thoughts regarding that day, Gus's attitude toward Cash's role in the company had genuinely changed. That was the face she showed him, that was the voice he heard when she spoke. Everything else was buried deep within herself, including the accompanying torment a secret of that nature evoked.

"Inevitability," Cash repeated slowly, and Gus realized he wasn't completely satisfied with the answer she'd given him.

She cleared her throat. "When are you planning to leave?"

Still frowning over Gus's evasive explanation, Cash said, "Monday morning. Nothing's open tomorrow."

"You could talk to Lloyd about it today. He's still at the shop, I believe."

"Yeah, he is." Cash started toward the door, but stopped after a few steps. "Gus, we can do great things with this company by working together."

He'd spoken tentatively, Gus realized, as though doubting that her recent cooperation had any staying power.

"I think we're in a day-by-day situation right now," she said. "You have long-range plans for the company, while

I'm already worrying about repaying that loan." She smiled to temper the observation.

"What I have are long-range hopes," Cash returned with a seriously intent gaze. She was changing, smiling instead of yelling, reasoning rather than presenting a biased opinion. Maybe he'd found that good side he'd admitted looking for, but how? If he'd caused this change of heart, what had he done?

Whatever the reason, it made Cash feel good, more like his old self. He grinned, and Gus saw some of the same sparkle in his eyes that she'd seen so often during his first days on the mountain. Her mouth twitched in automatic response, though her smile wasn't nearly as bright as Cash's.

She sighed when he left the office with a bounce in his step and leaped off the porch in one jump rather than using the stairs. In some ways he was like a little boy, she thought, an idea that was immediately reinforced by Cash going around the back of the office building and returning a minute later with Doodles on his heels.

The pup yipped and danced around his master's boots as they headed across the compound to the shop. The sight cheered Gus, and there was no denying the warm affection she felt for the duo.

She rested her chin in her hand and stared out the window. Going along on Cash's shopping expedition could produce some very intriguing results. Was that what she wanted? Eating together, traveling all over the state, staying in motels? If there was anything between them, wouldn't a week of that much togetherness bring it out?

But what if Cash took it the wrong way? Despite what he'd said about not touching her again unless she begged, he would probably make love to her without a whole lot of prompting. As she'd already decided, however, chemistry wasn't love, and deliberately inviting an affair just wasn't her style.

Besides, she was needed here. Sighing again, Gus picked up her pencil.

* * *

By that night Cash's nerves were jumping. He was so keyed up about his plans for him and Lloyd to leave before dawn on Monday morning, he wondered how he would make it through a long Sunday.

With darkness and everyone gone except him and Gus, the mountain was as silent as a tomb. Cash tried to read, but finding concentration impossible, he left the apartment and went outside. The only lights came from his windows and Gus's. An owl hooted nearby. A quarter moon hung in the sky and looked like pure gold against a velvety black background. The tall trees surrounding the compound created a sense of isolation.

Walking around the office building with Doodles trailing along, Cash settled himself on the front porch steps. The apartment lights weren't visible from there, nor were Gus's windows, and the darkness was so thick it took a minute for his eyesight to adjust.

He leaned back with his elbows on a higher step and thought about next week. Having newer and better equipment was a thrilling prospect. So was touring the equipment dealers and making the actual purchases. He chuckled softly, because until recently he never could have imagined himself getting all pumped up over something so prosaic as shopping for logging trucks. Not that a logging truck was a minor purchase. From the information he'd gathered from various dealers, he'd be spending a great deal of money.

It wasn't the money thrilling him, and it wasn't even the equipment. It was the involvement, the decision-making, the sense of belonging. He was taking roots in this mountain, sinking deeper into its lush, moist earth with each passing day.

He thought of Gus and felt an immediate stirring in his groin. If he could come up with even one slightly plausible reason for doing so, he would knock on her door. Not to make another pass. He would keep his promise about no more passes if it killed him. But his ragged, restless spirit tonight demanded company, another voice, a little conversation. Hell, he'd even consider playing cards, which he abhorred, if he had someone to play with.

"Someone to play with," he murmured aloud. The trouble with that speculation was, it wasn't cards he wanted to play with Gus. Today she'd been wearing an emerald-green blouse, which had brought out the green in her eyes. Her smile seemed lodged in his brain, as though it were the only smile he'd ever seen that was worth remembering.

Why was she suddenly nicer? Did she like him better than she had before? If so, why? Was her remark about inevitability the truth? The *only* truth?

Sensing movement in the black trees to his right, Cash sat up and peered at the area. Someone was there, walking toward the cookhouse, and there was only one other someone besides himself on the mountain tonight. When the light came on in the kitchen of the cookhouse, he got up. Not hurrying, he began a route that would take him around the cookhouse to the back door.

First there was a window, though, and he could see Gus inside. As was usual after dark, she was wearing a robe. Obviously she'd come for a snack, because she seemed to be deciding between apple pie or chocolate cake, with both sweet treats sitting on a table.

On impulse Cash rapped on the window. Gus jerked around. Her eyes were wide, her hand at her throat. Realizing that he'd scared her, Cash hurried to the door and went in. "Sorry about that. I just wanted to let you know I was out there."

Gus gave a shaky little laugh. "Guess I didn't think about you wandering around in the dark." She pulled the sash of her robe tighter. "Um...would you like something to eat?"

"Looks like your sweet tooth might be acting up," Cash said while grinning at the two desserts on the table. "I wouldn't mind a piece of that pie."

"Fine...uh, fine." Flustered because she wasn't dressed— though Lord knew Cash had seen her in much less than a robe before—Gus darted to a cabinet for two plates.

While she cut the pie he went to the refrigerator. "Want some milk?" he questioned while holding the gallon jug.

"I have milk at the house." Gus smiled weakly. "I planned to take something back."

He hid his disappointment. "Sure, I understand." After pouring one glass for himself, Cash put the jug of milk back into the refrigerator.

Gus picked up her plate. "Well...see you tomorrow." At the door she looked back to see Cash sitting down with his pie and milk. The silent throbbing of the place seemed suddenly pressuring. What the hay, she thought, throwing caution to the wind. "Would you like some company?"

Cash leaped to his feet. "I sure would!" He pulled the only other chair in the kitchen over to the table for her. Gus sat down, already regretting her impulse. She'd come over for something sweet to take back home and eat by herself before going to bed. Instead she was seated across a table from the only man who had ever reached her sexually, and if wearing a nightgown and robe weren't enough to shake her aplomb, she could always remember that there wasn't another human being for miles.

He rushed to pour milk for her, and brought forks and napkins to the table. She could eat fast and break this up within minutes, Gus decided, smiling her thanks for the glass of milk, fork and napkin.

"Listen," she said with her head cocked. "Is that Doodles I hear outside?"

Cash got up again. "I forgot he was out there. He's letting me know about it." The second Cash opened the door, the pup ran in.

"He really is adorable," Gus said around a bite of pie.

Cash resumed his seat. "Will you keep an eye on him while I'm gone next week?"

"Yes, of course. Is he housebroken yet?"

Cash nodded. "There's an occasional accident to deal with, but for the most part, yes."

"Then he can sleep in my bedroom," Gus announced.

"Lucky Doodles," Cash replied solemnly, though the corners of his eyes crinkled teasingly.

It was more of a reminder of her misstep than Gus thought necessary, spoken in jest or not. Mandy's excellent apple pie suddenly tasted like sawdust, though she forced herself to swallow and pretend complete indifference about the remark.

Her reactions weren't quite clever enough to escape Cash's notice. "Don't be embarrassed," he said quietly. "It happened, Gus." He wanted to say it could happen again very easily, that it *would* happen again if she gave the slightest sign. But the words remained only a thought in his own mind.

Gus's eyes were on her plate. "I think I've had enough pie. I wasn't nearly as hungry as I thought." She started to shove her chair back.

Cash's hand darted across the table to capture hers. "Why do I keep making mistakes with you?" Her gaze jumped from his hand holding hers to his face. "Tell me, Gus. If you understand the pull I feel toward you, explain it to me."

His voice was husky with emotion and affected Gus more strongly than his grip on her hand, as did the shimmering heat in his eyes. He was so vitally handsome, with features she could find no flaw in and eyes as blue as the summer sky. His shirt seemed glaringly white under the kitchen fluorescents, and was stretched smooth across his wonderfully masculine shoulders and biceps.

Did she love him? The question arose in her mind and wouldn't go away.

"Tell me," he repeated in a ragged whisper.

She opened her mouth to speak, but there was nothing there except that frustrating, unnerving question: *Did she love him?* She settled for a mumbled and barely coherent "I know even less about it than you do."

His hand moved on hers, enclosing it into a firmer grasp. "But you're not denying there's something between us."

"How...could I?" she whispered. "You're the only man...since my divorce. You're the only *other* man besides my ex-husband."

The information hit Cash like a massive dose of adrenaline. He got up and moved around the table. "Gus... damn." He spoke thickly and urged her forward.

She shook her head. "You said you wouldn't do this."

"I know what I said. Sometimes I talk like a damned fool. Gus, don't you realize what's happening with us?" Again he tugged on her hand in an attempt to bring her closer. He wanted her to take the final step between them, to do it because it was what she wanted, not because he was pressuring her again.

"It's the isolation," she whispered hoarsely, reaching for straws to explain the mounting tension. "That's all it is."

He rejected that idea with a snarled, "Like hell that's all it is. Don't lie to yourself about this, Gus. It's too important. You just admitted I'm only the second man in your whole life. That has to tell you something."

What did he want her to say? Her mouth was so dry she wondered if she could speak at all, and her mind was a confusing cloud of disconnected, meaningless phrases. Surely he didn't expect her to speculate out loud with him, to join together in some sort of embarrassing quest to unearth the reason they had made love one rainy afternoon.

"Cash . . . please," she managed to croak while she made an attempt to free her hand.

He held on. "Talk to me, Gus." One yank and she would be in his arms, and the urge to do it was becoming stronger by the second. He was unmercifully aroused. Not by the shapeless robe covering her beautiful body, but by her, her eyes, her mouth, her hair.

His eyes narrowed. What were her private hang-ups? Gus had some very straitlaced traits in business. Was she the same way with personal relationships? Was that the reason he was only the second man in her life? He refused to believe he was only the second man to notice her, which meant she had turned down all the others. So what did she want, avowals of undying love before committing herself to a relationship?

"Do you want me to say I love you?" he questioned. "Would those words make our need for each other all right?"

Her eyes registered shock and incredulity. "I am not try-ing to worm any such declaration out of you!" She jerked her hand. "Let go of me!"

He obeyed, reluctantly, and exactly as he'd thought, she whirled and ran for the door. Muttering under his breath he stayed on her heels, and when she opened the door he closed it again with one hand over her head.

He didn't move away, but stood there virtually sur-rounding her, his hand above her head and his body crowd-ing hers. She didn't try to turn around, but spoke, disdainfully she hoped, with her back to him. "You're only proving you're bigger and stronger than I am, which I think we both already knew."

He replied to the back of her head. "Maybe I'm proving we can't be alone together for long without some very ex-plosive feelings developing between us."

"Only when you push for an advantage."

"Is simple conversation pushing for an advantage?"

"The topics you choose to bring up do not come under the heading of 'simple conversation.'"

"Maybe that's because nothing is simple with you, Gus." Cash moved closer and closed his eyes to savor the heady sensation of his body against hers. He dipped his head to press his lips into her hair, and groaned softly at the intox-icating scent filling his nostrils. "Gus," he whispered.

Her knees felt about as useful as two globs of peanut butter. She was melting inside—everything internal seemed to be oozing together into one misshapen lump of super-heated clay. One fact was glaringly clear: Her imagination hadn't made something powerful and magical out of an or-dinary encounter their first time together. The same feel-ings were upon her again, destroying her will, altering her negative opinion of empty, irrational affairs of the heart, which under less influencing circumstances she preferred thinking of as uncontrollable eruptions of lust.

That's all this was with Cash. Certainly that's all this was *for* Cash. His reference to love was insulting. *Do you want*

me to say I love you? Would those words make our need for
each other all right?

It was demoralizing to realize if he had just said it, *I love*
you, Gus, instead of asking those oh, so telling questions,
she probably would have believed him and everything *would*
be all right.

She felt his left hand creeping around her waist and then
his breath on her scalp as he whispered urgently, "Turn
around, Gus. Turn around and let me kiss you."

A shock wave moved through her traitorous system. It
took all of the pitiful supply of strength she could muster to
shove his hand away and mumble, "No kisses."

His whole body moved against hers in the most seductive
way possible. She could feel his chest, his thighs, his belt
buckle and what was below it. "You want to be kissed," he
whispered. "You want exactly what I want."

Gus closed her eyes. He was ruthless and determined to
have her cooperation. She wasn't afraid he would force her
with brute strength, but she was afraid he would win if she
didn't get him away from her.

She furtively cleared her clogged throat. "Your ego is
astounding. All I'm feeling right now is utterly ridiculous."

Cash's head came up. "That's not true. Don't you think
I can tell what you're feeling? Your body is as hot as a little
furnace right now, and you're trembling."

"You bet I'm hot," Gus retorted. "Hot under the collar,
and if I'm trembling it's from outrage. I can't be nice to you,
can I? You're just waiting for me to relax my guard so you
can puff up and assume I'm panting for your body. Well,
think again, Cash. That one encounter we had did not give
you a lifelong hold over me, and maybe you'll realize it one
of these days."

Her cruel words struck Cash like a fist. Deep down he
knew she was lying. Her heat wasn't from anger, nor were
the tremors of her small body. He'd experienced Gus's anger enough to recognize the symptoms, and she didn't stand
and shake from anger, she yelled.

She'd talked about proof. He'd give her proof. With a grim set to his mouth, he took her shoulders and turned her around. Gus hadn't expected any such onslaught, and her mouth opened to lambaste his bloody gall. Instead her lips were sealed by his and the fury got stuck in her throat. She tried to escape his arms, but he merely clamped her to himself in a tighter hold.

And then he kissed her, thoroughly, possessively, with his lips and his tongue, and his body moving against hers. He kissed her until she was limp and whimpering and hanging on to him, until her lips were soft and malleable and obeying the commands of his. He kissed her until his own legs were unsteady and the desire raging through his system was more torment than pleasure.

Then Cash raised his head and looked at her. Her eyes were glazed, her mouth was wet and sensually swollen, and her fingertips were dug into the front of his shirt. He had conquered her objections and it was stunning to realize he might always have this power with Gus. Once he got her past her own stringent morality, she was a sensual, passionate woman. It was what he'd done before, kissed her into submission, kissed her into wanting what he did.

He could see reason returning to her eyes. He had two choices, kiss her again or let go of her. His aching body demanded another kiss and anything else he could lead her in to, which right now felt like the gamut of sexual escapades. But the strangest reluctance was churning his emotions and slowing his reflexes. Kissing a woman into submission wasn't really anything to be proud of. What the hell had he proven, other than something he'd already known, that kissing Gus could make them both a little bit crazy?

An enormous tenderness overtook Cash's passion. "I...I'm sorry," he whispered huskily.

Gus blinked at him. She felt his arms dropping away, his hands sliding from her back.

"Like I said, I keep making mistakes with you," Cash mumbled. He took her arm in his hand. "Come on, I'll walk you to the house."

She stumbled along as though drunk, trying to grasp what had just happened. He'd kissed her without mercy, and when she became mindless and clinging to him, he had stopped everything. There was no logic to it, no sense.

The lights from the front windows of the house spilled out over the porch. Cash led her up the stairs and opened her door. "Good night, Gus."

Disbelievingly she stared at him deserting her so abruptly. "Did that scene in the cookhouse do something for your ego?" She threw the words at his retreating back.

"What?" Cash turned around. "I don't want to fight, Gus."

Why did you stop? Why did you kiss me like that and then just stop?

Her anger vanished as quickly as it had jolted her. "Neither do I," she said wearily, and turned and went into the house.

But within the privacy of her home and with the lights off, Gus stood at the window and stared out into the black night. Her arms came up and curled around herself, as though she were constructing a shield. She knew now, and the knowledge was the most painful of her life: She was in love with Cash Saxon, who was fulfilling her earliest prophecies about him by proving to be the bane of her very existence.

However he felt about her, she was in love with him. It was the cruelest of all the blows she'd received since Cash's invasion of her beloved mountain.

Ten

By Sunday morning Cash had altered his departure plans. A long, inactive day with Gus being the only other person in camp didn't seem at all wise. Truthfully he didn't know what was, or if wisdom had the slightest bearing on the feelings Gus was arousing in him.

At any rate, it seemed best to avoid her today. He telephoned Lloyd at his home and asked him if he could leave for Portland today instead of tomorrow morning. Lloyd openly conferred with his wife and then agreed. Cash told him he'd pick him up in an hour.

Throwing some clothes into a suitcase, he mulled over his options with Gus: He could either knock on her door and tell her about his change of plans in person, or he could leave her a note. Facing her this morning was a disheartening prospect. He'd behaved like a jerk last night, and that wasn't the first time. Why couldn't he keep his damned hands off her? Why did he keep trying to prove something with Gus?

Disgustedly Cash slammed the suitcase shut and snapped the latches in place. Leaving a note was too cowardly. Before he could change his mind, he carried the suitcase out to the Wagoneer and headed for Gus's house.

Standing on her front porch, he knocked on the door. After a minute he knocked again. Finally he opened the door and yelled, "Gus?"

The house was silent. Frowning, Cash pulled the door closed and looked around the compound. Gus's pickup was in plain sight, so she hadn't done another disappearing act.

After checking the cookhouse and then the other buildings, Cash adjusted that opinion. He glanced at his watch. Time was passing, and he'd told Lloyd to expect him in an hour.

It took another ten minutes to put Doodles, along with food and water, into his outside pen, then go into the office, scribble a note, return to Gus's house and tack it to her front door.

He drove away considering Gus's absence as the same kind of avoidance he preferred today. She couldn't have gone very far on foot, but she probably hadn't wanted to see him this morning any more than he wanted to see her. The two of them were playing hide-and-seek like a couple of kids.

This couldn't go on. When he got back from this shopping expedition, he and Gus had better sit down and thrash everything out.

Gus entered her house by its back door. The long hike to the cave and back had cleared a lot of cobwebs from her brain, and she felt much better than when she'd crawled out of bed this morning. The cave had several different names in the area. Some called it Chinaman's Cave, others called it White Granite Cave. Mostly Gus thought of it as *her* cave, because it had been a favorite childhood haunt. Situated on the very edge of Parrish-Saxon land just before the terrain rolled into government property, the shallow, dry cavern had been a marvelous place for a little girl to play and do her daydreaming.

She'd done some daydreaming today, too, sitting within the mouth of the opening and gazing at an endless view of trees and sky. Today, however, her thoughts hadn't been those of a child. Today she had pondered the complexities of adult relationships, the intricacies of business and the loneliness of being without family. Every subject seemed to lead to the same question: What did she want from the rest of her life?

Children...yes. Another marriage...possibly. Financial security...it would be nice. Cash Saxon...oh, Lord!

Whenever Gus's thoughts landed on Cash, a debilitating weakness moved throughout her body. There was no longer a reason to debate her feelings for Cash. Having little comprehension as to why she would fall in love with an overbearing, egotistical man, who was her biggest threat to a peaceful future as far as the business went, carried absolutely no weight. She loved him. She loved him as she had loved no other person in her entire life, even her father, and God knew she had adored Big Jim Parrish. It was no wonder that her marriage had failed. How could it not fail when she hadn't felt even a fraction of the love for Larry that she now felt for Cash?

Gus recognized the enormous difference between loving someone and being in love. The feelings she had now seemed embedded in her very soul and disturbingly permanent. Being in love was not a pleasurable sensation. Rather, she felt jagged inside, and incomplete. Her bruised spirit demanded relief while her mind sought solutions. Connecting with Cash on some level, preferably honest conversation, seemed sensible.

Today being a Sunday and relatively free of responsibility was opportune. The crew wouldn't be returning until late afternoon. She certainly didn't plan to ask Cash right out how he felt about her, but never had they spent any time together just being themselves. That was the image in Gus's mind now, maybe a drive together, or merely sitting in the same room without animosity over the company, talking about whatever came to mind.

During the hike back to camp Gus's resolve strengthened. She wasn't adverse to making the first move toward an emotionally closer relationship with Cash, though it was possible his feelings for her were strictly physical. If that was the case she could be in for some long-term heartache. But facing her own feelings was a major first step; understanding his was an obvious second.

Inside her house, Gus went immediately to her bathroom for a shower. She took her time. Her day had begun early and other than the nervous pounding of her own heart, there was no reason to hurry.

An hour later she could make no further improvements on her appearance. Her hair was as perfect as she could arrange it, her makeup was as she liked it, subtle but accenting her eyes and cheekbones, and her outfit was casual and becoming, a favorite green and white skirt and blouse with a delicate floral pattern.

Her pulse was faster than normal, but she knew she had to do this. She had to knock on Cash's door and let him know with a smile and a few well-chosen words that she wasn't angry about last night, and that she would like to spend the day with him. Then it would be up to him.

Gus was still standing in front of the bathroom mirror. Her fingertips rose to her mouth as a vision of Cash laughing at her efforts, or telling her he wasn't interested, battered her senses. Her resolve weakened and all but disappeared.

Then the image vanished and she remembered last night, and their romantic interlude. It *had* been romantic. It *hadn't* been only lust. She realized now the element that had so mystified her at the time had been true affection for each other, she was positive of it.

Giving her hair a final pat, Gus drew a deep breath and left the bathroom. She walked through the house with renewed determination and opened her front door. Closing it behind herself with her gaze on Cash's apartment windows, she crossed the porch and went down the stairs.

Doodles began yipping in his outside pen. Gus smiled in fondness for the pup. She was about halfway between her house and the office-apartment building when she noticed the vacant compound. Cash's Wagoneer was gone!

Her heart nearly exploded in her chest. He was gone? Wildly Gus ran to the front of the office building and then stood there with her mouth open. He was gone. Where? Why?

This scenario hadn't occurred to her. Her courage was bolstered, as was her determination, and he was gone. For how long? Could she maintain her level of readiness for this bold move for several hours?

Dejection set in. Turning, Gus slowly walked around the office building, giving the blank apartment windows disbelieving glances. Doodles was jumping around behind the wire fencing, doing everything a pup knew how to do to gain Gus's attention.

He finally got it. Sighing heavily, Gus moved aside the makeshift wire gate and let Doodles out. "Where did your master go?" she asked drolly as she stooped to pick up the puppy. "Too bad you can't talk, little buddy."

Well, her plan was in ashes. Gus's gaze swept the vacant compound. Already her enthusiasm was waning. Already doubts were stacking up. What would she have said to Cash anyway, *Hey, sport, I've been thinking it over, and I've fallen in love with you. Isn't that a hoot?*

"It's a hoot, all right," Gus muttered as she lowered the wriggling puppy to the ground. Her disappointment was not rational. Cash had every right to go somewhere without her knowledge. But waiting all day for him to return was an unnerving thought. She'd been pumped up and ready for that honest confrontation; now she was losing confidence.

The first thing she'd do was get out of this dress. There was always book work to occupy her weekends, as dreary as that idea was. Gus started for her house, with Doodles following.

That was when she saw the piece of paper hanging on her front door. Instinctively she knew what it was; intuitively she knew she wasn't going to like it.

Hurrying up the steps, she snatched the paper from the door.

Gus,
Decided to leave for Portland today. Lloyd's going with me. Sorry about last night, even sorrier about talking you into bed that day. We're business partners and nothing else. Maybe, as you said, that fact will sink in someday. Thanks for watching Doodles. I'll be calling. Cash.

Gus read it a second time, then crumpled the paper in her fist and blinked at the tears in her eyes. She went into the house, tossed the wad into a trash can, hurried down the hall to the bathroom and washed the makeup off her face.

Never again would she dwell on ridiculous thoughts of being in love with Cash. Never again!

Cash called on Monday evening. "How're things going there?"

"One of the men quit," Gus replied calmly. "The State Employment Service is sending out someone tomorrow to take his place. Other than that everything's fine. How're you and Lloyd doing?"

"Great. I think we've found the dealer to do most of our business with. We haven't made any specific decisions yet, but Lloyd's excited about this company's inventory."

"That's good."

"Gus... about the other night."

"Forget it," she said evenly. "I have."

"You got my note."

"Thanks for leaving it." *Thanks for setting me straight, you snake!*

"I wanted to talk to you before I left but you were gone. Where'd you go?"

"For a hike. Don't worry. The note was more than adequate." She had retrieved that accursed note from the trash can and taped it to her bathroom mirror. It was the very best reminder she could ever have of Cash's true nature. If he ever put his hands on her again, he was going to get a dose of *her* true nature.

"I'll call again tomorrow night."

"Thanks for the courtesy. Goodbye."

In a way Gus was relieved that things had worked out as they had. At least she knew now where she stood with Cash. He found her physically attractive and convenient. She was, after all, the only woman on the mountain. Other than Mandy, of course, who was old enough to be Cash's mother and would probably clout any man alongside the head who tried anything funny.

That was what *she* should have done the first time Cash had come on to her, the first time he'd grinned that sexy grin at her, for that matter. It seemed ludicrous now that she had actually been remorseful because he wasn't laughing as much, or because his blue eyes had lost their teasing sparkle. Who in hell cared if he laughed? She wasn't laughing.

On Tuesday morning the new man arrived. "Name's Lee Hensley," he announced with a sassy grin, obviously beaming because his new boss was a woman.

Gus groaned inwardly. Another sexy grin she didn't need. Lee Hensley was young, tall, lanky and good-looking. Beneath his saucily set cowboy hat was pale golden hair. His eyes were almost as blue as Cash's, and Gus could see that the guy was just positive that he was the greatest thing walking around on two feet. The male ego never failed to astound her.

"Are you experienced?" she questioned bluntly.

"Very."

The smooth response annoyed Gus. "I'm talking about the woods. Tell me what jobs you've done *in the woods*." The grin faded on Lee Hensley's face, which thrilled Gus no end. She'd run into this same situation before—a new man, full of vinegar and instantly seeing action because of his boss being a fairly attractive woman.

After a few minutes of recitation, Gus was satisfied with Hensley's background. The State Employment Service usually sent out good men and Hensley was no exception. He had worked in the woods all his life and was qualified to do any job she set him at.

"All right, you're hired," she told him. "You can leave your rig parked here and get on the bus with the crew."

Hensley looked over his shoulder. "Which one of those guys is the foreman?"

"I'm the foreman," Gus said coolly.

"You?" The grin reappeared. "This job just keeps getting more interesting."

"Ever been hired and fired in the space of two minutes before?" Gus asked.

"Uh . . . no."

"Then wipe that silly grin off your face and get on the bus. This job is no more *interesting* than any other you've had."

"Hey, you don't need to get mad."

"I'm not mad, Mr. Hensley. What I am is your boss *and* your foreman. We'll get along just fine if you remember that."

The infamous grin flashed. "Can't blame a guy for trying."

While Hensley sauntered over to the bus, Gus thought of that phrase. *Can't blame a guy for trying.* It was the excuse every horny man used for hitting on a woman, and was, undoubtedly, the one she'd hear from Cash if she ever actually succeeded in pinning him down on why he couldn't keep his hands in his pockets instead of on her.

Can't blame a guy for trying, Gus. Yeah, she could almost hear him saying it, probably accompanied by a charming, boyish grin, partially guilty, partially proud. In Cash's case he hadn't only tried, he'd succeeded. It was demoralizing to admit just how well he'd succeeded. Even he didn't fully comprehend the extent of the pleasure she'd attained in his arms.

And he never would if she had anything to say about it.

The days passed. Cash called every evening. Conversations revolved around trucks and chain saws, prices and trade-in values, delivery dates and more prices. Gus could tell that Cash was being very cost-conscious, which she appreciated. Their evening telephone discussions were amiable if not particularly friendly. Certainly nothing of a personal nature was mentioned after that first call.

By Saturday evening Cash had everything wrapped up. The newly purchased equipment would be delivered to the mountain on Monday. "Lloyd and I will be back tomorrow."

That announcement sent a cold chill skittering up Gus's spine. The week without Cash underfoot had been healing. Tomorrow everything would change. "Fine," she said tonelessly. "See you then."

Gus put down the phone with a tight, uneasy frown. Weekends were becoming a burden. During the week she was too busy to worry about Cash's fatal charm. But tomorrow would be another long day, and what time would he be arriving? In the morning, the afternoon? Lord, she'd be on edge all day.

Unless she made herself scarce. Dare she resort to that same ruse again? They had both used it. Why else had Cash left a day early if not to avoid her?

Still, she couldn't start leaving the mountain every weekend. Saturdays and Sundays were when she did the book work. Most of today had been spent at her desk, and she had planned to finish up in the morning and then relax for the remainder of the day.

Gus got up to pace. She wouldn't be doing much relaxing tomorrow, not with Cash either on the horizon or in plain sight. But this was going to be the norm for the rest of her days. How was she going to deal with it? Why wasn't he old and ugly? Or married. Dammit, why wasn't he married?

That question opened up a whole new avenue of thought, which kept Gus well occupied and vexed until bedtime.

Exactly as Gus had predicted, she was keyed up all day Sunday watching for Cash's Wagoneer. She was going to be calm when he arrived, she swore. Calm and collected. She might do a lot of stewing and pacing in private, but Cash was never going to get a reaction out of her again—not anger, not passion, not anything.

That vow wore a little thin when the sun went down and everyone else had returned to camp and Cash was still absent. He had managed to ruin another Sunday for her, Gus thought disgustedly as she went through her nightly ritual of shower, nightgown and robe. But who had really ruined it, Cash or herself? Had anyone forced her to hang at whichever window was handy to stare out at the empty compound?

She snapped off the house lights and sat in the dark. If he arrived tonight and had the audacity to knock on her door, she simply wasn't going to open it.

An hour later every light in every building had been extinguished. Gus was getting a little uneasy. He'd said he would be back today, and today was over. Something was wrong.

Her phone rang at ten. Gus jumped up to answer it, switching on lights as she went. "Hello?"

"Gus?"

It was Cash. There was music in the background, and laughter, the unmistakable rosy, cozy sounds of a tavern. Gus's stomach muscles tightened.

"I'm in Hamilton. Just dropped Lloyd off. We had some car trouble, but Lloyd finally got it fixed. Pays to travel with a mechanic." Cash chuckled. "Anyway, I'm going to grab a sandwich and be on my way. I thought you might have noticed I wasn't there and didn't want you worrying over nothing."

"I wasn't at all worried," Gus lied.

"Oh. Well, that's good. Gus, our new equipment will be delivered tomorrow."

"So you said."

"I'm anxious for you to see it. I think you'll be pleased."

"I think I'll save the praise until after so much debt and expenditure proves profitable."

The cutting remark set Cash back on his heels. "You do that, Gus," he drawled into the phone. "Maybe you won't mind my excitement, though I'll do my best to keep it to myself."

"You do that, Cash," she replied, throwing his sarcasm back in his face. "In the meantime, why don't you go and soak your damned head!" She slammed down the phone, then stared at it, appalled at her outburst. Maybe he should have called earlier, before she really had started worrying, but any call at all had been considerate. What was wrong with her?

Wailing aloud, Gus ran for her bedroom, where she threw herself across the bed. She couldn't do it. She couldn't act calm and collected with Cash when everything he did or said drove her up the wall. If this was love, heaven help all people hit by the same virus. Besides, she didn't love him, she hated him.

Pulling herself up, Gus punched her pillow. She could not go through fifty-two weekends like this one every year for the rest of her life. Maybe she should move to Hamilton and commute as the crew and Mandy did. For a few moments the idea appealed to Gus. Living in town did have its advantages.

Except the second she left the mountain, Cash would undoubtedly move into her house! Into this wonderful log house that her father had built with his own two hands. Her father had done everything on this mountain, erected the buildings, created a business, operated it and worked hard every day of his life until illness befell him. Why should those Saxons own half of it? Why should Cash have as much say about this house as she did?

Recalling his question about how her father and his grandfather might have met to form their partnership, Gus mulled it over. It wasn't something she'd ever questioned before, but it seemed monumentally important now. Wouldn't she just love to find some scrap of paper, some notation in an old journal, *something,* to prove the Parrishes deserved the company and the Saxons did not?

The storage room contained at least a dozen boxes of old records. She wouldn't know where to begin, but what if there was crucial information in one of those cartons about the onset of the company, something she could wave in front of Cash's face and announce, "I'm moving to town, and you do not have my permission to live in my house."

It was getting late and four-thirty in the morning came very quickly. But she couldn't resist at least a cursory peek into some of those boxes.

Gus was thrilled to see that most of them were dated. Pushing and pulling them around on the shelves, she managed to free the one with the oldest date. Inside were a stack of yellowed file folders and several old journals. She thumbed through the folders and was elated to see one labeled Saxon Correspondence.

Positive she was on to something, Gus took the Saxon folder to the kitchen table and sat down to go through it. The papers in it were fourteen years old. She read copies of her father's letters to a Mr. Gerald Saxon, and Mr. Saxon's letters to James Parrish.

Near the bottom of the stack was a letter that shook her very foundation.

> *Dear Jim,*
> *I've been considering your offer very carefully. I like your ideas, Jim, and the map and detailed plans you sent me for selective harvesting of my timber appear sound and sensible. As you can see, I have enclosed a deed to the land, which will be the first asset of our partnership. Your contribution of equipment and labor to remove and sell the timber will make us equal partners. Yes, I know you mentioned the land's value as being much higher than your contribution, but that's something I intend to overlook. I value your knowledge of the timber industry and rely on your good judgment for a long and profitable future.*
>
> *Your friend and partner,*
Gerald Saxon

Gus sat there, stunned. The land had come from Gerald Saxon, no doubt Cash's grandfather. My God. All this time she'd been thinking her father had owned the land first. Fourteen years ago she had been old enough to know what was going on, and she probably would have if Big Jim hadn't been so biased on the role of women in business, particularly the logging business.

But she had lived here longer than fourteen years! Frantically Gus went through the rest of the folder. Additional correspondence told the tale. Her father had been working for Gerald Saxon—*working for him*—and had ultimately proposed the partnership arrangement that had endured through the present.

Gus closed the folder. Instead of finding something to put her one up on Cash, she had found just the opposite. Her father might have done all the work, but he never would have owned any portion of the mountain without Gerald Saxon's generosity. It was an awful blow.

Well, she could still move to town, but she certainly couldn't demand that Cash stay in that dreary little apartment rather than take possession of this house.

Listlessly Gus put away the folder and went to bed. Her choices now were to suffer with what she had, or to take Cash up on his offer for one of them to buy the other out.

She cried herself to sleep. The thought of borrowing money to buy him out gave her cold chills, and she couldn't even consider selling him her share of the company and leaving the mountain forever.

As he'd pointed out so arrogantly, they were both stuck.

Eleven

————

Cash saw the lights in Gus's house when he drove in, but he was so beat he could barely get himself into the apartment and into bed. He and Lloyd had spent hours on that back road—a shortcut of Lloyd's—working on the Wagoneer's fuel pump. Lloyd had finally gotten it repaired, but that breakdown coming at the tail end of a hard week and in the middle of a long drive had sapped Cash. He would see Gus in the morning, and maybe then have the strength to ask her why she'd told him to go soak his head, though nothing she said should surprise him anymore.

When his alarm rang at four-thirty, he groaned and forced himself out of bed. A shower knocked the cotton out of his head, and he dressed and went over to the cookhouse for breakfast.

Walking in, he stopped dead in his tracks. Gus was sitting at a table with some young guy he didn't know, and she didn't look like she minded the guy's lecherous grin one little bit, either.

Jealousy ripped through Cash's system, tensing his mouth and hardening his eyes. He had turned his back for one lousy week, and some S.O.B. had immediately moved onto his turf.

His turf. Gus was his, not that yellow-haired pansy's with the toothy grin. He felt like jerking him out of his chair and...

Whoa! This wasn't like him. He'd never jerked anyone out of a chair in his life. Warning himself to cool off, Cash sucked in a breath and walked over to the counter with the food. Today he piled a plate high with whatever he could reach without giving a thought to what he would be eating. He wasn't thinking about food at all, just about getting his plate filled so he could sit down at that table.

Balancing the overloaded plate and a mug of coffee, Cash walked over to Gus's table. "Good morning."

She'd known he was coming. She had seen him walk in and spot Lee sitting with her. Lee Hensley was an incorrigible flirt. No matter how bluntly or how often she put him in his place, he kept coming back for more.

It hadn't occurred to her until Cash walked in and turned green right before her eyes that he might not like Lee following her around. The idea was startling and suggestive. If Cash was actually jealous wouldn't that indicate deeper feelings for her than he'd put in that note?

On the other hand, men were territorial creatures and all he could be feeling was possessiveness. If that was the case, he was going too far. Not feeling up to this sort of silly game at five in the morning, Gus gave him a look that told him to stop glowering.

"Good morning," she coolly replied. "Cash Saxon, Lee Hensley. Lee, Cash is your other boss."

Lee partially stood up and offered his hand. Cash looked from it to the man's face and saw the challenge lurking in Hensley's eyes. He wanted Gus and wasn't above letting his "other" boss know it. "Sorry," Cash said curtly. "My hands are full."

Gus winced. Cash's rebuff was so obvious it was embarrassing. He sat down. Lee sank back to his seat. Gus cleared her throat.

Cash took a sip of coffee, blatantly eyeing Hensley over the rim. "Apparently you're working here now."

Lee nodded. Gus was aware of the masculine tension at the table, which made her grit her teeth. How dare these two square off because of her! "Gus hired me last week. Tuesday, wasn't it, Gus?"

"Tuesday," she concurred icily. Just as coolly she said to Cash, "You remember my telling you that a man quit, don't you?"

"I remember," Cash growled. "So, Hensley, what job has Gus got you doing in the woods?"

"I've been skidding," Lee replied. Gus could tell he was weighing the situation and deciding it might be prudent to back off. She was positive of it when he said, "Maybe I should move to another table. You two probably need to discuss business . . . or something."

"Good idea," Cash said before Gus could intervene. He stared right into her glaring gray-green eyes while Hensley got up and took his plate and cup to another table clear across the room. "Ain't he just a doll?" he drawled the second the man was out of earshot.

"Don't be absurd! How dare you presume so much?" Gus looked around. There wasn't a snowball's chance in hell of carrying on a private conversation in here. She could practically reach out and touch the man at the next table, and any fool could see everyone in the room had an ear cocked. "Just drop it," she hissed under her breath.

"Are you going to the woods this morning?"

"Don't I always?" Gus retorted.

"And you always come back, don't you?" Cash drawled with heavy sarcasm.

Gus flushed three shades of red. He wasn't talking about the woods in that nasty remark. She got up and picked up her plate. "I'm finished, and you're getting damned close."

With that quixotic exchange between them, Gus dropped her plate on the counter and strode from the dining room, slamming the door behind her as she left. She was steaming, mad enough to chew nails. Heading for the office, she slammed that door as well.

In the dining room Cash forced food down his throat. The men all seemed to be talking about something else, but there was no ignoring the curiosity in the air. He'd made a fool of himself, marching in here like a little general and throwing down the gauntlet. He glanced over at Lee Hensley and felt his gut tighten. He still didn't like him. The guy was hot on Gus's trail, and if she had a brain in her head she'd know it. The thought of her with another man sickened Cash. What was he, falling in love with her or something? Yes, he'd thought about commitment with Gus before, but love? The real McCoy? The genuine article?

He got to his feet and brought his plate to the counter. The men were still eating. He had maybe ten minutes before Gus left for the woods, and it was ten minutes he was going to use to get a few things straight between them.

Gus saw him coming, barreling across the compound as though geared up for battle. That was fine with her. She was furious, and this whole fiasco had gone as far as it was going.

Cash walked in. Gus was standing with her hands on her hips and evil in her eye. "Don't start yelling," he warned.

"I'll yell all I please! Just who do you think you are, going in there and making a scene like that?"

"That jerk wants your body, lady! Maybe you're too naive to see it, but every man in that room knows it."

"I *know* what that jerk wants. Contrary to your insulting opinion of my intelligence, Cash Saxon, I'm not stupid and I'm not naive! Do you actually believe I haven't run into men who think they're God's gift before? What about you? Aren't you the perfect example of masculine conceit? What have you been doing from the minute you stepped foot on this mountain, if not trying to trap me in some dark corner?"

His face grim, Cash moved closer. "What I did was different."

"Oh, yeah? Tell me how? At least Lee's been confining his lechery to transparent grins and adolescent remarks. *You* sweet-talked me into bed!"

"Wasn't very damned hard to do," Cash growled.

"Thank you very much," Gus shouted. "That was precisely the insult I needed to put a stop to this ridiculous partnership! I'll buy you out, mister, the second I can raise the money!"

Cash put his face right in hers. "Like hell you'll buy me out! I'll buy *you* out!"

"I'm not selling my father's company!"

"Well, what makes you think I would sell my grandfather's company?"

"Because you said you would!"

"What I said, you noisy little pip-squeak, is that one of us should buy the other out! I wasn't talking about selling, I was talking about buying!"

"Don't you dare call me names, you...you arrogant *Saxon!*" Gus swung her right arm so wide and hard, she nearly toppled herself with the breeze. Instead of connecting with his insolent face, however, she found her wrist trapped in a viselike grip. "Let go of me, you conniving reptile!" she screeched.

"Good God, is there no way to shut you up?" Cash suddenly thought of a way and jerked her forward. His mouth crashed down on hers without even a hint of tenderness. He ground her lips with his, and brought her up against himself in a crushing embrace.

She couldn't move or yell or do anything but stand there and bear it. He liked the silence, and he liked having her in his arms. He especially liked the whimper that finally came from deep in her throat and the way her body started molding to his.

He backed them both up to lock the door, never breaking the kiss that had become hot and needful and hungry, and then over to the window to yank down the shade. In the back of her mind Gus knew what he was doing. In the back of her mind she knew the men would notice the drawn shade and poke each other in the ribs about it.

But the back of her mind wasn't doing the sizzling; that was happening in all of the private places of her body, in all of those spots she'd always possessed but had hardly been aware of until this arrogant Saxon brought them to life.

Controlling her emotions with Cash was a laugh. Why had she wasted the energy in telling herself otherwise? He could infuriate her with one word or arouse her with one kiss. She was suddenly as greedy as he was and didn't give a damn about it, either. She could take as well as he could. She could grope and tease and torment, and walk away afterward without a backward glance, the same as him.

She unbuttoned his shirt and pressed her mouth to the hot skin of his chest while unbuckling his belt. He was as busy with her clothes, opening buttons, pushing her shirt apart, unhooking the back of her bra. Disheveled, both of them, breathing hard and seeking kisses and more and more intimacy, they managed to open jeans and push them out of the way. Gus's jeans hung off one foot, Cash's sagged just enough.

He lifted her, brought her clean off the floor, and growled, "Put your legs around me." She did it. He slid inside her. Gus gasped and threw her head first back then forward to bury her face in his throat. Neither moved, though Gus was trembling.

"Look at me, Gus."

It was a command, spoken in a low, gravelly voice that she barely recognized. She lifted her head to look into his eyes. Their sensual depth and dark color compounded the thrills in her body. "You're...crazy," she whispered. "We're both crazy."

"Crazy for each other. Don't tell me we don't have something special." He moved his hips, withdrawing and advancing in a seductive slide.

She moistened her lips with her tongue. "Do that to me," he demanded raggedly. Her arms were around his neck. Her head dipped forward slightly, until the tip of her tongue could reach his lips. He shuddered when he felt it circling his mouth. "Baby...if you only knew," he rasped.

"I do know," she moaned, moving her bottom to meet his thrusts. Making love this way was insane when there was a bed in the next room. Maybe they really were a little bit crazy, both of them. But nothing in her life had ever been so exciting. The love she had finally admitted for Cash was overwhelming her now, rising in her chest and throat and causing a roaring in her ears. She wanted to say it, the words were close enough to taste.

But dare she let go of her last shred of autonomy? Hadn't she started losing individuality and independence the second Cash set foot on the mountain? Their battles had not been shallow confrontations for a spectral control, but rather personality clashes of the deepest order. Confessing love, even at this most emotional of times, would be like handing him the keys to a city. Unless he said it first and with undoubtable sincerity, she wouldn't be able to suppress her own feelings.

But Cash was thinking of making love, not of being in love. His mind was as feverish as his body, focused on the erotic pleasure Gus was giving him. The same heat, the same intense need he was feeling was in her eyes. She was so hot, so small, the most incredibly arousing woman he'd ever known, and making love this way was wild. He knew he wasn't going to last for long, but from Gus's rapt expression and throaty moans, she was with him.

Cash watched her face while they moved in frenzied harmony. Distinct thoughts weren't possible with so much sensation, but he was aware of the passionate glaze in Gus's beautiful eyes, and the light sheen of perspiration on her skin. Until meeting Augusta Parrish, he'd been a sane and sensible guy. But if this sort of blissful delirium was a sign of nuttiness, he'd take it over sane and sensible any day of the week.

It wasn't possible to express in words what he was feeling, and he didn't even try. Gus took offense to everything he said anyway, so what was the point? They were communicating just fine right now, and he was more than willing to maintain a sexual relationship on one hand and their business partnership on the other. It might not be the most perfect arrangement between a man and a woman, but with Gus's volatile temperament it was probably all they'd ever have.

Becoming aware of the trembling in his legs, Cash moved to a wall and put his back against it. Slowly he slid down to the floor, bringing Gus with him. Maybe he would never let go of her, he thought when she snuggled against his chest. Her fingers wove into his hair for a passionate flurry of kisses.

He lifted her and brought her down again. "I've never made love like this before," Gus whispered.

"Don't feel like the Lone Ranger, baby. Neither have I."

She got the hang of it very quickly for a novice. They both did. In seconds their emotions had reached the explosive stage. Curling her hands around his head, she hung on. "Cash...oh, Cash," she cried.

"Stay with me, baby," he mumbled thickly.

She could do nothing else. He was filling her, again and again, and making her greedy. Even with their awkward position they had found the perfect tempo. This time Gus didn't have to wonder about what would happen next, and she reached for the glorious sensations with every cell in her body. The peak was blinding. Rivulets of intense pleasure seemed to follow every vein and nerve she possessed, leaving behind a wake of weakness. Slumping against Cash while trying to catch her breath, she dimly realized that he, too, was weak and still.

If he was ever going to mention love, now would be the time. Gus's cheek was pressed to his chest, and she listened to the hard pounding of his heart while preparing herself for that special moment.

What she heard made her own heart nearly stop in shock. "I don't want Hensley working here."

She raised her head. "What?"

"Hensley. I don't want him chasing after you."

"The man does not chase after me!"

"Don't defend him, Gus, not after this."

Gus swore if she cried now she would despise herself till her dying day. "You are without a doubt the most insensitive, unfeeling, callous jerk I've ever had the misfortune of knowing!'' Clumsily she scrambled away from him, realizing suddenly that they both looked like they'd been tossed around by a tornado. Their clothes were half-on, half-off. Cash's hair was standing on end, obviously from her ardent and admiring attentions. If either of them had the slightest inclination toward modesty at this debasing moment, they may as well forget it.

Red-faced, Gus jerked the shambles of her clothing around in a frenzied attempt to cover herself.

''What in hell's eating at you now?'' Cash growled. Getting to his feet, he hauled up his jeans.

''You are!'' Gus yanked and pulled and finally managed to untangle her jeans and panties enough to pull them up. ''One would hardly think the first words out of your mouth after...after... Oh, just forget it!''

Cash grabbed her by the arm. ''You don't think I should dislike Hensley? What would you prefer I do, look the other way when he leers at you? Forget that notion, Gus.''

''Well, you're not going to fire him because of your own disgusting imagination!'' Gus shook off his hand to hook her bra and straighten her shirt. ''Lee's darned good in the woods, and that's all the interest I have in the man.''

Cash was regarding her broodingly. What had she expected after their lovemaking? She'd nearly socked him when he'd mentioned the word *love* before. Had her attitude on that subject changed during his absence?

''How come you told me to go soak my head on the phone last night?'' he questioned.

Gus's eyes darted to his. ''Uh...I can't remember.'' Reasonably put together, she started for the door. ''I'm going home for a few minutes.''

''Gus, do you want to talk?''

She turned. ''About what?''

''About us,'' he replied sharply.

Her gaze slid from his. ''Do you?''

''Can't you give me a straight answer?''

Dammit, why couldn't he just instigate a conversation without making a big deal out of it? If he wanted to talk about them, why not just say so instead of putting the burden and responsibility of a personal discussion on her?

"The only answer I've got right now is that the men have gone to the woods and I haven't," Gus finally said.

Cash's mouth tensed. "Would you rather wait here for the truck deliveries and have me go to the woods this morning?"

"Hardly. I wouldn't even know if the right trucks were delivered. You stay here." Hurrying to her house, Gus cursed the negligence that both Cash and herself had just displayed by not using protection. She knew what her problem was—falling in love with the wrong man—but what was his?

In her bedroom, she tore off her clothes and furiously threw them across the room. The tears didn't start until she was in the shower. Frustration set her whole body to trembling. How could she have so little control with Cash? Being in love wasn't a license for this sort of misconduct, and her sexual indulgence wasn't going to make him fall in love with her, either.

After drying off, Gus dressed quickly while her mind searched for signs, things Cash had said and done during their acquaintance that could be construed as personal and important. Each and every event could either indicate deep affection or merely another bout of lust, she realized as her self-disgust grew. Maybe she was even interpreting her own lust as love. Her sex drive had never overpowered her common sense before, so she had no past experience on which to judge her present response to Cash. Apparently despising her weakness for him wasn't going to destroy it, but neither could she go on and on with this sort of excruciating situation.

Today at breakfast, in front of the entire crew, Cash had openly laid claim to Gus Parrish and she had allowed it. Her initial anger couldn't possibly have fooled anyone, not when she and Cash had disappeared into the office and pulled down the window shade.

So now everyone knew. But what did they know exactly? That their two bosses were having an affair? Gus cringed at the thought. Facing the men was going to be a trial. She was even apt to hear some good-natured ribbing, as a few of her men were prone to teasing with a lot less provocation than they'd received this morning.

Well, she could handle the teasing and knowing looks. That certainly wasn't her biggest problem. Cash was. She, herself, was.

So, just what was she going to do about it?

The trucks and the other purchases Cash had made were delivered midafternoon. Lloyd came out of the shop and Mandy came out of the kitchen. The three of them stood around and admired the new equipment until the bus arrived with the logging crew. Gus drove up in her pickup right behind it.

She got out with her mouth open. Cash walked up to her with both pride and anxiety on his face. "What do you think?"

Gus was staring at the shiny red-and-chrome trucks. "They're...they're beautiful. All the same color. You didn't tell me."

Cash heard his name being called. "I've got to show those drivers where our old trucks are parked so they can take them back to the dealer." He gave Gus a hopeful look. "Don't go away."

The logging crew members were walking around the trucks and exclaiming over them as proudly as though they had paid for them out of their own pockets. Gus approached one truck and saw the sign on its door—*Parrish-Saxon Logging Company*. She stopped and bit her lip, worried that she was going to shed about a bucket of tears right there in front of everyone. Cash's generosity with the company name was very touching.

But after reading the sign on the truck's other door, the threatening tears evolved into dismay, for as plain as day, for all the world to see, it said *Saxon-Parrish Logging Company*. And every truck was the same.

It took over an hour for the deliverymen to take possession of the old trucks and be on their way. The company men had wandered off, probably to take their showers before one of Mandy's good suppers. Gus couldn't bring herself to desert the red trucks. She climbed up into the cabs, and monkeyed with the complex shifting levers, and wiped nonexistent dust from the dashes and fiddled with the CB radios.

"So, Gus, what do you think?"

She looked down to see Cash standing there. Regardless of the equipment's accompanying debt and her own torn-up emotions about this morning, the trucks were wonderful. "I love them," she said simply.

Cash heaved a silent sigh of relief, then gave the huge truck a fond once-over. "So do I." Gus's reaction had been a major concern. Her attitude was even more positive than he'd hoped for, and at this moment warmth for her expanded and blossomed within him. He held up his hand. "Let me help you down."

Gus took his hand and managed the precarious climb down without too much awkwardness. "By the way," she said once her boots were firmly on the ground. "What about those signs?"

"I thought they were rather...uh, tactful."

Gus's gaze went to the nearest sign. "A little peculiar, though, don't you think? Maybe confusing?"

Cash thought a minute. "I guess I was trying to be fair and went a little overboard."

The signs suddenly struck Gus as funny. Her laughter surprised Cash, but it was contagious and he began laughing with her.

"What do you think people will say when they catch on that each side of our trucks say something different?" Gus gasped.

"Probably that we're a couple of nuts," Cash replied, laughing. "Did the men notice?"

"Not that I heard."

It occurred to them both at the same time that this was the first time they had laughed together. Gus's laugh faltered.

"Don't back off," Cash said softly. "It was fun to laugh together. This is an important day, Gus."

She wasn't sure if he was referring to their shared laughter or to what they had shared that morning. Suddenly infused with the heat of memory, Gus wondered if this was the moment to speak frankly. Or romantically. To tell him that though she had fought against feeling so much for him, she had lost the battle and needed to hear something from him about his feelings.

Then again, he could merely be thinking of the newer equipment, Gus decided with an inward sigh. Certainly the arrival of the trucks had created a landmark day for the company. Pondering her unusual situation, she gazed off into the distance.

"What are you thinking?" Cash asked. There was so much going on with him and Gus. Standing there in her dusty work clothes amid the gleaming red and chrome trucks, she presented a complex picture of dedicated business partner and appealing female.

"I'm thinking of...a lot of things," she replied thoughtfully, vaguely.

"Of this morning?"

"That's part of it," she admitted quietly, though her cheeks got pink.

Cash realized that he hadn't been bothered by Lee Hensley this afternoon. Apparently his unreasonable surge of jealousy this morning had passed, thank goodness. Walking around with that sort of ache in his gut was a horrifying prospect and completely senseless. If Gus wanted another man, his throwing his weight around wouldn't change her mind.

But he didn't believe that was the case. Gus Parrish and Cash Saxon were a pair. Maybe not a totally matched pair, as a pair of socks were. Maybe a pair more like a right and left hand were. And maybe they would never decide which of them was dominant, which was the right hand and which was the left. But he'd be willing to bet that if a threat to either one of them should suddenly appear, the other one would leap to his or her partner's defense.

The two of them were no longer in the process of getting involved with each other, Cash concluded in a flash of enlightenment. They were already involved, just about as deeply and steadfastly as could happen to a man and a woman.

"I'm thinking of this morning, too," he said in a husky undertone, which was the God's truth. He'd thought of little else all day. "Gus…" And just like that a brand-new and exceedingly harsh question hit him: What did he have to offer Gus? The business? She already had that, with all of its potential and possible pitfalls. Could he give her financial support? Yeah, right. He'd have to do better than that one, he told himself. How about loving her as he'd loved no other woman? But what else would his love be right now but a burden for her?

"What, Cash? What were you going to say?" Gus could tell it was something important and spoke anxiously.

"Uh…" Except for knowing he couldn't talk about love and marriage until the company was on its feet and he'd proven that his ideas for its success weren't all pipe dreams, Cash's mind was a confusing blank. "It was…nothing."

Gus didn't believe him. Something crucial and serious had been going on behind his incredible blue eyes, and she wanted to know what it was.

"You were thinking about us," she dared to accuse.

Stunned by the far-reaching consequences of his own thoughts, Cash sought refuge and privacy behind a deliberately cocky grin. "I was thinking of how much I'd enjoy washing your back and other delectable portions of your anatomy in the shower."

Gus's expression reflected her shock. "That's a lie!"

"Honey, I never lie about washing a woman's back," Cash drawled teasingly.

Expecting too much never failed to hurt a person, Gus thought as a wave of utter agony seared her senses. How many times was she going to give Cash an opening to destroy her? Wasn't his note still taped to her bathroom mirror enough of a reminder of the shallowness of his feelings?

She was too hurt even for tears. This was the end.

But she wouldn't waste her breath in telling him so. In fact, the only way to prove to Cash that their shoddy affair was truly over was in performance. He'd get the message in time.

Her smile was cool and as distant as the stars. "Thanks for the offer, but I prefer showering alone. See you at supper." She walked away.

It wasn't going to take any great length of time for Cash to get the message; he already had it. Gus wanted more than quick thrills from him, which was both gratifying and disturbing.

"Gus!" he yelled.

She stopped and turned, praying he wouldn't be able to detect her horrible inner turmoil. "What?"

Cash caught up with her. "I figure it'll take about a month for us to know if my projections are accurate."

Grasping the significance of his statement was impossible in her present state of chaos. She was looking for his heart, and all he could think of was getting naked in the shower with her. How much plainer could their differences in attitude be?

"Meaning?" Gus's voice wasn't exactly pleasant and certainly not friendly. It was how she intended to speak to Cash from now on. As for anything else, anything the least bit personal or hinting of intimacy, he was in for a rude awakening.

"I'm hoping next month's financial picture will be a lot better than it's been." He stopped talking, because what else was there to say right now? The trucks were bought and on the mountain. All they could do now was work the hell out of them and pray that his predictions *were* accurate.

And yet he wanted her to know he loved her. The problem with that idea was that he wanted her to know it without putting it into words. Surely she understood how strongly a man felt about having at least a modicum of financial stability before proposing marriage to a woman, didn't she?

Instead of saying the words, Cash put the message into his eyes. He tried to put it into a touch, as well, by bringing his hand up to Gus's face.

She leaped back as though burned. Startled by her excessive denial of a rather ordinary expression of affection, Cash narrowed his eyes. "You do understand why I mentioned my hope for better profits, don't you?"

"It's what you've wanted all along, isn't it?"

"Yes, but—"

"Then I understand perfectly. I really have to go and clean up. Mandy will be ringing the dinner bell."

"You don't understand at all, you little fake," Cash muttered as Gus ran across the compound toward her house. It was as though she couldn't put distance between them fast enough.

"But you will," he added grimly after she had disappeared through her front door. "You will."

Twelve

Gus could hardly believe the change in Cash. Wearing his new steel-toed boots, he spent all day, every day, in the woods with the men. Then, minus the boots, he spent all evening, every evening in the office with a pad, pencil and calculator. What really got Gus's goat was that he didn't stop working just because a weekend rolled around. The trucks were washed and polished inside and out, and any small imperfection immediately repaired. Lloyd was admittedly less busy these days, though Cash kept him hopping on servicing the new equipment.

When the trucks could no longer be improved on during Saturday and Sunday, Cash hiked through the woods with Big Jim's map, familiarizing himself with the mountain. "Probably getting to know every tree," Gus peevishly muttered to herself when trying to digest what was happening.

It might be petty to feel annoyed at so much dedication, but Gus couldn't help herself. Why had she worried about her and Cash being alone on the mountain during weekends? He was barely visible, for one thing, and for another, when he was in sight he spoke to her in only the politest of terms. What had happened to all of that passion he'd had for her? Now he acted as if she was one of the guys!

Well, that wasn't a hundred percent true. At times she caught his eyes on her and suffered a torturous hot flash from the intensity of his gaze. The passion was still there but tightly controlled. Why?

While the office lights burned at night and Cash was computing yet another pad full of income and cost projections, Gus paced her house and worried about her own perversity. When he'd been making passes, she had fought both him and herself to ignore them. Now, when he wasn't, she constantly stewed. If that wasn't contradiction in its most elementary form, nothing was.

In more rational moments, however, Gus knew very well what was eating at her with Cash's new regime: She loved the big jerk and always would. His devotion to the company would be heartwarming if he was nothing more than her business partner, but he seemed to have attained an almost godlike stature in her thoughts. Her initial opinion of Cash Saxon had done such a total turnabout, it was astounding.

The situation became even more stressful for Gus as the summer progressed and she found herself getting hot and cold from the mere sight of Cash's long, lean body, or his shock of dark hair that fell so beguilingly over the right side of his forehead. Entering the dining room with him occupying one table or another, usually sitting with a group of men and picking their brains about some phase of the logging process, made her feel that her own feet weighed fifty pounds each. Going to the woods and seeing him so deeply engrossed in the operation, or running into him in the office when their schedules happened to overlap, never failed to make her heart skip necessary beats and then plunge into a crazy rhythm that made the natural act of breathing a supreme effort.

She was suffering the traumas of a lovesick teenager, which she deemed disgusting and immature. Any twenty-eight-year-old woman who wanted a particular man that badly should have the gumption to pin him down and find out what *he* wanted. If it weren't for those sizzling looks he gave her every so often, she wouldn't be in such a quandary, Gus argued in her own defense. But the hot, sexy looks continued, and so did her perplexity.

One evening she dashed over to the office to write a check that was needed first thing in the morning. One of the men had requested a payroll advance before the normal payday due to a family emergency. His wife would pick up the money in the morning, he'd told Gus that afternoon, and she had promised to have the check ready and waiting at first light. The whole thing had slipped her mind until she was getting undressed to put on her nightgown and robe.

Recalling her promise, Gus hastily rebuttoned her shirt and grabbed a flashlight for the walk to the office. The lighted windows evidenced Cash's presence, but what else was new? she thought wryly as she opened the door and went in.

He laid down his pen. "Hi."

"Hi." Gus went to the file cabinet for the checkbook. She explained about the advance check and sat down at the second desk to write it. Cash always used the one by the window unless she was using it first, but she had stopped worrying about that trivial sin some time ago.

Writing a company check was practically second nature to Gus, but the fine hairs on the back of her neck seemed to be standing on end from Cash's stare, and she made a mistake and had to void the check. Clearing her throat, she started filling in the blanks of a second check.

His stare was driving her crazy. Her eyes lifted from the checkbook. "See anything interesting?" she bluntly asked.

"I think you know what I'm seeing."

Gus made a production out of looking behind her. "Nothing there. You must be looking at me." Her spurt of courage amazed her, but if she didn't challenge Cash soon, she would be a candidate for the funny farm. "Am I interesting, Cash?"

His countenance darkened. "Don't tease, Gus."

"Why not? Maybe you need teasing, Cash. Maybe you need ... something."

"And we both know what that something is, don't we?" he asked in a dangerously soft voice. In the next instant he picked up his pen. "But not tonight."

The last few seconds had opened a door for Gus. She frowned, feigned concentration on the checkbook and instead tried to nudge the door further open. Things started falling into place: Cash had put their personal relationship on some kind of ambiguous hold!

And then she remembered his comments about his hopes for the company's financial future the day the new trucks had been delivered. He'd said something about making more profit and then asked her if she understood what he meant. She told him she did!

But she hadn't.

She did now. My God, was it really that simple? Was he actually staying away from her until the company was making money? What if it *never* made any real money? What if it just kept poking along the way it always had, turning a small profit but never quite achieving the success Cash had envisioned in his first projections? If the financial history of this company was any measure, they could both be old and gray years before they got rich!

Gus groaned right out loud and put her left elbow on the desk and her forehead in her hand.

"What's wrong?" Cash instantly questioned.

Gus dropped her hand. "Nothing I can't handle." It was a private vow, because this was something she was *definitely* going to handle. She tore out the check and stood up to put away the checkbook. "It's ready except for your signature. Please sign it before you leave."

Cash slowly got to his feet. "Are you sure you're all right?"

Gus's mind was racing, devising schemes and discarding them with the speed of light. She stopped at the door. "Um ... there is something. Are you planning to work on Saturday?"

"Probably. Why?"

"Because it's... it's my birthday!" she blurted. It was a big fat lie and seemed like a painfully thin excuse for asking him to goof off rather than work. But she had started the ball rolling and had to keep it going. "I was just thinking of... oh, I don't know... maybe a picnic. I suppose you'd rather work than go on a picnic, right?"

"Saturday's your birthday? Gus, I'm sorry. I didn't know."

She smiled indulgently. "Of course you didn't know. How could you?"

"A picnic, huh?" Cash rubbed the back of his neck a trifle uneasily. "Well, sure, why not!"

Guilt whipped through her. She'd done several things since meeting Cash that wouldn't survive a close scrutiny, such as snooping in the apartment when he wasn't there, and saying nothing about that old correspondence she'd found proving that Cash's grandfather had owned the mountain before the Parrish-Saxon partnership had even been formed. An out and out lie about a birthday that wasn't due for another six months was probably her worst crime, though.

Gus lifted her chin. On Saturday she would confess everything. *Everything!* Waiting until the company showed a big profit was just too damned crass. Did Cash think she was money hungry? If he loved her it was time he said so. They could make the company profitable together. Or starve together, if that's the way it worked out.

"I'll take care of the picnic lunch," she told him.

"Don't forget to include a birthday cake." Cash smiled. "And how many candles?"

"Uh... too many." Gus pulled open the door. "See you tomorrow."

The idea of a picnic was growing on Cash. He moved to the door just as Gus went through it. "You know, I can't even remember my last picnic. Must have been a long time ago."

"Good night." He was standing in the lighted doorway, but Gus didn't look back. Pointing the flashlight's beam at the ground, she made a beeline for home. Already she was worrying about Saturday. Maybe she'd bitten off more than she could chew. How would she begin with Cash? Confessions were much easier to contemplate than carry out.

By the time Gus was ready for bed, her courage had returned. This had to be done. She wasn't going to procrastinate until the financial statement showed a larger profit. If she accomplished nothing else on Saturday, Cash was going to hear that she did not equate love and money.

Saturday finally arrived. To Gus's disappointment Mother Nature wasn't cooperating with her planned "birthday" party. The sky was heavy with dark clouds and the region was obviously in for some rain. Canceling the picnic wasn't an option, however. Gus wanted Cash's undivided attention, and it seemed judicious to get him completely away from the compound and the business to avoid distractions.

Gus raided the cookhouse kitchen and came up with a satisfactory lunch, with the main dishes being fried chicken and potato salad. She filled a wicker basket with the food. There was no cake, though she included several of Mandy's cinnamon rolls and some fresh fruit. Her sizable stack of picnic accoutrements included eating implements, a tablecloth and a blanket to sit on.

She was just finishing up when Cash came in. He looked a bit startled. "All of that for a picnic?"

Gus nodded solemnly, though there was laughter in her voice. "Everything you see here is necessary for a proper picnic."

His expression became teasingly tolerant. "You probably know more about what's needed for a proper picnic than I do. All right, I'll do the loading. Which vehicle?" He grinned. "Assuming we're taking a vehicle, that is."

"We are, but I don't care which one. You choose."

Cash picked up an armload and left. Realizing she had overlooked beverages, Gus filled a thermos with coffee and another with water. She looked around, wondering what else she might have forgotten. Excitement made her a little giddy. She had put on her denim skirt instead of jeans that morning and taken pains with her makeup and hair. She wanted everything to be perfect.

But she realized the imperfection of her plans when Cash returned singing, "Happy birthday to you, happy birthday to you, happy birthday, dear Gussie, happy birthday to you."

She shaped a sickly smile. Maybe she was going too far. "Cash..."

He was still smiling. "What?"

It was hard to look at him. "Today isn't...what I mean is..." With a deep breath, she dived in. "Today isn't my birthday."

"Tomorrow?"

"Uh...no. Not till February."

"Then why...?" Cash looked at the remaining picnic gear, then back to her. "I don't get it."

"I wanted—" Gus searched for something logical "—you to take a day off."

He frowned. "You made rather elaborate plans to accomplish it, wouldn't you say?"

"Rather devious plans," Gus admitted in a low voice.

"Do you want to tell me why?"

Gus didn't want this conversation taking place in the cookhouse kitchen. "Will you still go with me?"

Cash's eyes narrowed on her. "Is it important to you?"

"I...have several things to tell you."

"And you can't tell me what they are right here?"

"I could," Gus said reluctantly. "But I'd rather talk elsewhere. I had planned to take you to my favorite place on the mountain."

Cash was thinking hard. Obviously Gus's picnic idea was supposed to create an opportunity to talk. Where that birthday scheme had come from he would never know, but there was desperation in her eyes that he couldn't ignore. Maybe a frank discussion was best.

Three weeks had passed since he'd decided to stay away from her until the company was on its feet, but that decision was difficult to live by when it meant battling his own harassing urges to touch her every time she was in reach. Not that complete candor would be easy. But surely he could make her understand that what he felt for her couldn't be taken to its logical conclusion until things were financially less stressful.

"All right," he said quietly. "I'll go."

Gus's relief was obvious. "Great. Thanks."

Together they carried the rest of the picnic gear outside. "I put the first load in the Wagoneer," Cash told her. Gus wondered if her honesty about this not being her birthday so early in the day had been prudent. Certainly it had altered their moods. Cash had turned sober and thoughtful, and all traces of laughter had vanished from her system.

Cash fit his armload and then Gus's into the back of his vehicle. Walking around the rig, he opened the passenger door and held it while she got in. "Thank you." Her lips felt a little numb, and her pulse was much too rapid.

Cash slid behind the wheel and started the engine. "Which direction?"

Gus laid out their route to the cave, which was farther away by road than by hiking cross-country. But she hadn't wanted to hike it today, not loaded down with backpacks, though the relaxation she had hoped to gain from her "elaborate plans," as Cash had labeled her efforts, wasn't exactly prominent at the moment.

"We're going to Chinaman's Cave," she explained, forcing a lilt in her voice. During the drive she kept talking about the cave, relating her childhood fondness for the place in enough detail to keep them occupied.

"You can park just ahead," Gus finally announced. Cash pulled over at a wide spot in the crude roadway. "It's just a short walk from here," she told him with her heart suddenly in her throat. What if she botched things so badly Cash took offense? Or what if he had nothing to say? What if she wrangled a confession from him that consisted of no more than an admittance of having once enjoyed their sexual activity?

By loading themselves down, they toted the picnic paraphernalia in one trip. It was uphill and they arrived at the cave winded. Cash laid his load on the ground and turned to look at the view. "It's beautiful up here."

"Come and see the cave," Gus urged. She went in first and then stood there proudly while Cash looked around.

"It's great, Gus." He placed a hand on the white rock wall. "Dry as a bone."

Their gazes tangled. "Well," Gus announced brightly. "I'll lay out the food. Are you hungry?"

"Sure," Cash replied agreeably. He was going to let Gus bring them to the point of this outing, though he was enjoying its intrinsic value. He'd seen dozens of beautiful spots on this mountain, and kept discovering more. But this place was special to Gus, which made it special for him.

Outside again, Cash took a look at the threatening sky. "It's going to rain, Gus. Maybe we should set up the picnic inside the cave."

"Good idea." Gus began spreading blankets on the ground at the mouth of the small cavern. "We'll eat here. Then if it starts raining, we can easily drag everything deeper inside."

Cash watched more than he helped. Watching Gus was a satisfying pastime. Well, not exactly satisfying, not when her every movement raised his blood pressure and made him remember how long it had been since their sexual collision in the office that one morning. It *had* been a collision, one he would remember for the rest of his life unless another of greater excitement occurred. It wouldn't happen with anyone but Gus, of that he was certain.

"Come and sit down." Gus patted the blanket and began taking food from the basket.

They ate while commenting about the view, the humid weather and the food. Each knew there was more in the air than rain, but neither brought up anything controversial. Cinnamon rolls and coffee finished the meal. Gus repacked the basket with their dishes and the leftover food. Her heart was beating wildly; the time had come.

She didn't look at him. Instead she kept her gaze on the endless view, which was lulling to her nerves. "I have a few things to tell you."

"So you said," Cash said softly. There was about two feet of space between them. Seated on the blankets, they were both facing the view.

"I . . . snooped through the apartment one day when you were gone."

Cash's head snapped around. "Not that I care, but why would you want to?"

"Because I was scared of why you were here. I don't know what I expected to find," Gus said on a rueful sigh. "Anyway, it's been on my conscience and I wanted you to know. There's something else. I looked through my father's old files hoping to find something to prove you had no right to claim fifty percent of the company."

Gus slanted her head to look at him. "Do you remember asking me how my father and your grandfather got together to form the partnership?"

Cash nodded. "I remember."

"Weeks ago I learned what happened from the correspondence in that file. Dad worked for a Gerald Saxon. He was your grandfather, right?" Again Cash nodded. "That's what I thought. Dad suggested the partnership. Gerald already owned the mountain."

"No kidding? Hey, that's great, Gus. I wondered . . ." Cash's enthusiasm waned. "What was your reason for not telling me about it right away? You knew I was curious."

"It wasn't in my best interest to tell you then," Gus admitted.

"And now?"

"I believe our interests are . . . compatible," she said in a husky voice. "Your right to be here is unquestionable, maybe more so than my own."

"Don't question your right to the company, Gus. I never have and I never will."

"No, you never did, did you?" she said softly. "I immediately saw you as a threat, but you never once intimated that I should assume second position. That was my biggest fear, you know."

Cash gave a short laugh. "Cutting you out of the business never entered my mind. Why would I hack off my own

right arm? You're the one who made the whole thing work."
He became reflective, looking out at the view again. "I
think we're making progress with the newer equipment, but
if my ideas end up hurting instead of helping, I'll have a hell
of a time forgiving myself. You had things pretty well under control just the way they were."

Gus's face registered amazement. "Are you questioning
your decisions?" That notion had never occurred to her.

"The decision to borrow money and buy better equipment was mine. You never would have gone out on a limb
like that without my talking you into it." Cash thoughtfully rubbed his jaw. "I still think it's going to work, but,
yes, I've been doing some questioning."

"And you're waiting for the outcome."

"Yes, I'm waiting," Cash concurred.

"Not idly. If there's the slimmest chance that hard work
will do it, you're going to make it happen."

Cash's head came around, and she felt the impact of his
eyes on her. "You sound like my working hard is a detri-
ment to the company. Is that how you see it?"

"Of course not." Gus drew a breath for courage. "But
you're loading one basket with all of your hopes, Cash.
What bothers me about that concept is that you've locked
my hopes into the same basket, and there they all lie, waiting and silent and just possibly deteriorating a little. For
certain there's nothing in there with them to make them
flourish."

She definitely had his attention. He was staring at her with
a rapt expression, and she could tell her analogy was sinking in. She moved closer and put her hand on his arm. "I
love you. Do you care?"

He swallowed. "My God, yes, I care. But . . ."

The enormous relief in Gus's system nearly destroyed her
ability to speak. But she managed around her clogged throat
and racing heartbeat. "Do you think I will love you more if
the company starts making money?"

Cash frowned. "Uh . . . I don't think that's what I had in
mind, no."

"Then reverse it. Do you think I will love you less if the company *doesn't* make more money than it's been doing?"

"Gus, you don't understand."

"You're right, I don't. Explain it to me, Cash."

The determination in her eyes set Cash's heart to pounding. She was very close, and her hand on his arm felt like a solid, irrevocable connection. It was how he'd been wanting the two of them for a long time, united in spirit, bonded by emotion.

But it was happening a little too soon. "I have nothing to offer you," he said gruffly.

"I have nothing to offer you," she said softly, and saw his eyes widen.

"You have *everything* to offer, everything I want!" he exclaimed. "I love you so much I can't see straight."

A sudden mist in Gus's eyes began clouding her vision. "But I have no money."

"My God, do you think that matters?"

Gus maintained her teary gaze. "What else can I think?"

"Don't compare...I mean, don't turn us around! A man should have . . . a man should have *something,* Gus!"

"You have precisely what I do, one-half of a struggling logging operation and one half of this mountain." She smiled tremulously. "You also have all of my love. Cash, I don't want to wait until the hopes in that basket become stale or too fragile to survive. Do you realize we could be having this same conversation a year from now? Two years? If the company makes money right away, wonderful. But what if it doesn't? Cash," she whispered, "delaying our future would be wasting an awful lot of precious time."

Inching closer to him, she slid her hand along the front of his jeans to his fly. "Do I have to seduce you to convince you of how much time we've been wasting?"

Cash's voice was thick with emotion. "Believe me, you're convincing me."

Gus hadn't planned any big seduction scene in this conversation, but it suddenly seemed like the most desirable of ideas. Bringing her mouth to his, she feathered kisses along his lips. "My final confession is about this," she whispered. "About making love with you. I told you I didn't like sex, but I didn't tell you why. It's because I—'' her whisper became even lower and huskier ''—never felt anything before. You make me feel so much, Cash. I didn't know such feelings actually existed beyond the imagination. Since that morning in the office, I've awakened a dozen times every night to remember and suffer. In short, my love, you unleashed a demon in me that refuses to be pacified without—'' she had been working down his zipper; her hand slipped inside to caress him ''—without this.''

In a fluid if hasty movement, Cash laid back on the blanket and pulled her on top of him. "I thought of this scene plenty of times," he growled. "But it was always me doing the seducing."

"That's because I let you do all the work in the past," she whispered. After a long and hungry kiss, she raised her head to see him. "Tell me you love me again."

"I love you, but I'm not sure love is an excuse for jumping ahead too quickly."

"I'll accept any reason for waiting except money. Can you give me any?" While speaking, she wriggled her hips in between his thighs.

"Not with you doing that, I can't." He stroked the sweet curves of her bottom. "I've laid awake nights, too. Don't think I haven't."

She teased his lips with the tip of her tongue, which she already knew made him a little crazy. "If we suffered our insomnia in the same bed, think of all the fun we could have."

"You're a witch," he groaned.

"A witch who's insanely in love." Sobering, Gus looked into his eyes. "I never thought I'd fall in love with you, but I did. We both caught the same bug, thank God. So...what are we going to do about it?"

Cash, too, had sobered. "Gus, if the company falls flat..."

"It's not going to, but say it did. I know I'd want to pick up the pieces and start over, and I could do it a heck of a lot easier if you were by my side." An adoring smile built on her face. "Not too many weeks ago I would have cut out my tongue before saying something like that." Her gaze moved over his remarkable features. "Damn, you're handsome, Saxon."

"Ah, Gussie," he sighed, and brought her head down to meet his hungry mouth. His kisses landed indiscriminately on her nose, her cheeks, her lips, and his hands never stopped moving. Elated because she was wearing a skirt, he began working it up.

His fever was highly contagious. Gus contracted it immediately and decided that further conversation could be delayed until later. He got rid of her panties while she unbuttoned his shirt, and then they spent long delicious minutes exploring each other's bare skin. "This time, no clothes at all," he growled.

"I couldn't agree more. Oh, oh, it's raining."

Laughing, they stood up to haul everything deeper into the cave. In the dry, warm space of the cavern, Gus pulled off her clothes while Cash shucked his. She became weak from just looking at him. "Like I already said," she whispered, "damn, you're handsome."

Grinning teasingly, he pulled her into his arms. "Maybe it's only my—" he meaningfully cleared his throat "—body you love."

"Let's say it was the first thing I fell in love with," Gus murmured. Her fingertips played across his lips. "On second thought, it was your mouth. The way you kissed."

His body was urging completion, but there was one more thing to say. His gaze captured hers. "You want us to get married, don't you?"

Gus's breath caught. "Yes."

"It's what I want, too."

She waited for more. "And?" After another pause she whispered, "Please don't have any more doubts. Cash, I love you so much. Earning a living is important, I can't say it isn't. But you can't deny we make a good team. We complement each other. You're imaginative, I'm conservative. It's a good balance."

Bringing her head to his chest, he rested his chin on her hair and stroked her back. His time in Oregon flashed through his mind, their first meeting, their arguments, their lovemaking, his determination with the company, his avowals to succeed.

Gus stirred in his arms. "Cash?"

With his forefinger he tipped her chin and looked into her eyes. "I love you, Gus. Let's get married."

Happiness rocketed through her, but she kept it at bay and searched his eyes. "I know I did my best to talk you into my point of view. Are you sure?"

"I don't want that basket of hopes to get stale, either, Gus. Fate forced us into our first partnership. Let's you and I choose our second. Yes, I'm sure. I've never been more sure of anything. Gus Parrish, will you marry me?"

She set the happiness free. "Cash Saxon, I would be proud and honored to be your wife."

"It's still raining," Gus murmured. Lying on one blanket and covered with the other, they were warm and cozy curled up together in the dry cave.

"You'll meet my brothers at Christmas," Cash said drowsily.

"Wonderful. I want to meet them. Are they coming here?"

"We agreed to a Christmas get-together, but we haven't yet decided on the place." He chuckled then. "What'll we do about the signs on the trucks after we're married?"

"That's easy. We'll have them changed to read Saxon Logging Company."

Cash hoisted himself up to an elbow to see her face. "That wouldn't bother you?"

Gus lovingly touched his cheek. "I'll be a Saxon, too, won't I?"

He thought a moment. "I think the signs should be changed, but how about Saxon and Saxon Logging Company?"

Gus smiled. "Remember when I called you an insensitive jerk? I take it back, my love. I take back every nasty thing I ever said to you."

"Then you like that idea?"

"I like *all* your ideas. I also like some of my own." Gus slid both of her hands under the blanket. "I'm getting one right now that you might like, as well."

He sucked in a breath. "Yeah, I like your idea just fine."

"I thought you might," she whispered.

Epilogue

After numerous long-distance conversations, the Saxon brothers decided to hold their Christmas reunion at the Kidd River Ranch in Montana. Cash explained the decision to Gus.

"First, Chance and Cleo's ranch house has bedrooms enough to accommodate everyone. Secondly, Cleo's daughter is only eight and Cleo would like Rosie to be in her own home for Christmas. Thirdly—" Cash grinned "—there should be snow in Montana and we'll have a white Christmas!"

Gus was already well-informed about Cleo and Rosie, and could hardly wait to meet Chance—the eldest brother—and his family. Rush, the youngest, and his bride, Valentine, would be traveling from Las Vegas, Nevada, for the celebration, another pair Gus was dying to meet.

The telephone calls had flown fast and furious for a while. "*You're* getting married? *I'm* getting married!" It seemed that each of the three Saxon brothers had met his ideal woman, and for the first time in years Gus genuinely worried about how she might look to other people.

It would have been nice to plan an elaborate, triple ceremony wedding, everyone thought, and they all discussed it through several calls. In the end, however, no one felt comfortable about leaving their respective businesses until Christmastime, so each couple said their vows with local friends in attendance.

On December 24, Cash and Gus boarded a plane for Helena, Montana. They were met by an elated party of five, Chance, Cleo, Rosie, Rush and Valentine. The rapport was remarkable. The women briefly envied each other's looks, then quickly formed a sisterhood. Meeting their husband's two brothers was daunting for only a few minutes, and everyone loved Rosie, the only child in the group.

But not for long. Cleo was pregnant and Chance was beaming all over the place. He announced proudly while holding Rosie's small hand in his, "Next spring Cleo and I will have *two* children."

"Chance really does love Rosie," Gus whispered to Cash at the first opportunity.

He squeezed her hand. "How could he not?"

The little girl's bright eyes made Christmas a special treat. Every room of the ranch house was decorated with something seasonal. There were pine boughs and mistletoe, a wonderful ten-foot tree in the living room, scented candles, wreaths and Santa and Mrs. Claus knickknacks.

But there was no snow.

Gus saw Cash talking to Rosie. "I'll bet you wish there was snow for Christmas, don't you, honey?"

"There will be, Uncle Cash," the little girl said solemnly. "You'll see."

Gus's heart nearly melted in her chest. To have a daughter like Rosie would be the height of happiness. She was beautiful, with long dark curls and huge blue eyes, though it was the little girl's sweet disposition that made everyone around her love her.

Guilt struck Gus. She had already attained the height of happiness! As Mrs. Cash Saxon, she should ask for nothing else.

But a baby, a child from her and Cash's love. How could wanting a child be too much?

Throughout Christmas Eve, while everyone ate the marvelous food Cleo had prepared, and listened to carols on the stereo, and realized again and again, joyously, that this room full of people was family, the subject of no snow came up repeatedly. Every time it did, Rosie said serenely, "But it will snow tonight. You'll see."

Once, when the three women were alone in the kitchen, Gus said, "Rosie is adorable, Cleo. Does she still believe in Santa?"

Cleo laughed. "I think she's at that stage where she's doubting Santa but can't quite bring herself to face the truth. I have to admit to encouraging the myth. Santa puts the merry in Christmas for children, don't you agree?"

"Wholeheartedly," Valentine said, and so did Gus.

In bed that night, Gus snuggled into her husband's arms. "I love them all, Cash. Do you think they like me?"

"Yes," he said without the slightest reservation. "They all think you're great, honey."

"I was worried."

"I know, but Chance and Rush told me that Cleo and Valentine worried about the same thing."

"But they're so beautiful! And friendly, and intelligent. Both of them."

"So are you, Gussie." His right hand began wandering. "You're my dream girl, sweetheart."

Gus laughed deep in her throat. "And this girl knows what you're dreaming about right now, too, doesn't she?"

"Hope so."

"How thick are these walls?" Gus whispered. "We get a little noisy, you know."

"They've all got better things to do then lie awake and listen for creaking bed springs," Cash said on a husky chuckle. "And Rosie's been asleep for hours." His hand went under his wife's nightgown. "I love you, Gus. There isn't one single thing in this whole world that could make me any happier than I am right now."

Gus bit her lip. "You know I feel the same. I love you more than I can say, but..."

"But what, honey?"

"A baby, Cash. I'd...like to have a baby." Gus stiffened with her announcement, because children was one subject they hadn't talked very much about. Admittedly they were busy. The company took up most of their time. But Cash's predictions and projections were proving to be factual. Saxon and Saxon Logging Company was making money, and its proud owners were constantly coming up with innovations and improvements to expand its base of profitability.

"I suppose a baby would create problems," Gus said wistfully when Cash didn't immediately respond to her declaration.

"Let's not worry about the problems, Gussie," Cash whispered. "Let's only think about the joy a child brings."

Gus's heart nearly stopped. "Then you agree?"

"I agree."

"Oh, Cash!" Gus turned in bed to fling her arms around her husband's neck. "I love you so much!"

Their lovemaking never failed to amaze Cash. Long after Gus was asleep, he laid there and counted his blessings. There was something a little mystical about all three of the Saxon brothers bravely marching out to face their fate after the death of their grandfather, and then meeting their life-partners in the first few weeks of a new and untried existence.

The Saxon family was growing. Thinking of Chance with two children brought a smile to Cash's lips; thinking of himself as a father filled his soul with gladness. Life was good.

An indistinct sound alerted Cash to someone moving around in the house. He knew who it was, as Chance had mentioned that he would be playing Santa around midnight so Rosie's presents would be under the tree when she got up in the morning.

Quietly Cash got out of bed, pulled on his jeans, shirt and socks and tiptoed from the room. He found Chance downstairs arranging Christmas gifts around the tree.

"Hi."

Chance looked up and grinned. "I tried not to wake anyone."

"I was still awake." Cash surveyed the pink-and-white, child-size bicycle and the dozens of other gifts under the tree. "It looks great, Chance. Rosie will be thrilled in the morning."

Rush came in. "Are both of you playing Santa?"

"All done," Chance announced. "How about a cup of cocoa?"

"Like Granddad used to make for us when we were kids and couldn't sleep?" Rush asked. "Do you know how to make it?"

Chance chuckled. "I use a mix, but it's not bad. Come on."

They silently trooped to the kitchen. It took only a few minutes to heat the water for the cocoa mix, then they sat at the table to drink it. This was the brothers' first solitary time together, and the camaraderie at that table touched all three men.

They talked quietly, each relating the events since their last meeting. The question they were all thinking about finally arose, stated by Chance, "Are we going to merge our respective business ventures into one entity?"

"I'll do whatever you two want," Rush stated.

"So will I," Cash said.

"Then we're still undecided,". Chance replied. "Should we leave everything as it is for another year?"

"Agreed," both Cash and Rush declared.

They laughed, because it was so obvious they were all contented with their vocations and lives. They talked about money, and their wives, and their hopes and plans for their business ventures.

Finally their second cups of cocoa were empty and the brothers were yawning. Together they climbed the stairs to return to their beds.

Cash silently opened and closed the door of his bedroom. Gus hadn't moved in the bed. He undressed and was about to crawl in beside her when his glance fell on the window. Outside a yard light on a tall pole burned, and its diffused rays kissed the windowpanes. Tiny speckles danced within the rays, and a sudden, bounding joy swelled in Cash's chest.

He moved to the window to see out. It was snowing. The minute flakes drifted lazily and the placid scene of falling snow touched Cash's soul. Rosie had been right, and his own youthful hope for a white Christmas had come to pass.

He got into bed and pulled Gus into his arms. She stirred sleepily. "Cash?"

"It's snowing, Gussie."

"Merry Christmas, darling," she whispered.

"Merry Christmas, my love." He smiled and closed his eyes. Life was *very* good.

* * * * *

SILHOUETTE® Desire®

"She's a no-good floozy out to ruin my son's name!"
—Lucy Dooley's ex-mother-in-law

OUTER BANKS

LUCY AND THE STONE
by Dixie Browning

When May's *Man of the Month,* Stone McCloud, was sent to North Carolina's Outer Banks to keep Lucy in line, he couldn't find a floozy anywhere on Coronoke Island. There was only a very *sweet* Lucy. Was she trying to wrap him around her ringless finger—and then do him in?

Don't miss LUCY AND THE STONE by Dixie Browning, available in May from Silhouette Desire.

MILLION DOLLAR SWEEPSTAKES (III)

No purchase necessary. To enter, follow the directions published. Method of entry may vary. For eligibility, entries must be received no later than March 31, 1996. No liability is assumed for printing errors, lost, late or misdirected entries. Odds of winning are determined by the number of eligible entries distributed and received. Prizewinners will be determined no later than June 30, 1996.

Sweepstakes open to residents of the U.S. (except Puerto Rico), Canada, Europe and Taiwan who are 18 years of age or older. All applicable laws and regulations apply. Sweepstakes offer void wherever prohibited by law. Values of all prizes are in U.S. currency. This sweepstakes is presented by Torstar Corp., its subsidiaries and affiliates, in conjunction with book, merchandise and/or product offerings. For a copy of the Official Rules send a self-addressed, stamped envelope (WA residents need not affix return postage) to: MILLION DOLLAR SWEEPSTAKES (III) Rules, P.O. Box 4573, Blair, NE 68009, USA.

EXTRA BONUS PRIZE DRAWING

No purchase necessary. The Extra Bonus Prize will be awarded in a random drawing to be conducted no later than 5/30/96 from among all entries received. To qualify, entries must be received by 3/31/96 and comply with published directions. Drawing open to residents of the U.S. (except Puerto Rico), Canada, Europe and Taiwan who are 18 years of age or older. All applicable laws and regulations apply; offer void wherever prohibited by law. Odds of winning are dependent upon number of eligibile entries received. Prize is valued in U.S. currency. The offer is presented by Torstar Corp., its subsidiaries and affiliates in conjunction with book, merchandise and/or product offering. For a copy of the Official Rules governing this sweepstakes, send a self-addressed, stamped envelope (WA residents need not affix return postage) to: Extra Bonus Prize Drawing Rules, P.O. Box 4590, Blair, NE 68009, USA.

SWP-S594

Coming Next Month from

SILHOUETTE®

Desire®

The next in the delightful

HAZARDS, INC.
series

THE PIRATE PRINCESS
BY
SUZANNE SIMMS

When Nick decides to take some vacation time on Key West, he never expects to get mixed up in Melina Morgan's zany plans to find her ancestor's long-lost buried treasure!

HAZARDS, INC.: Danger is their business; love is their reward!

Rugged and lean...and the best-looking, sweetest-talking men to be found in the entire Lone Star state!

In July 1994, Silhouette is very proud to bring you Diana Palmer's first three LONG, TALL TEXANS. CALHOUN, JUSTIN and TYLER—the three cowboys who started the legend. Now they're back by popular demand in one classic volume—and they're ready to lasso your heart! Beautifully repackaged for this special event, this collection is sure to be a longtime keepsake!

"Diana Palmer makes a reader want to find a Texan of her own to love!"   —*Affaire de Coeur*

**LONG, TALL TEXANS—the first three—
reunited in this special roundup!**

**Available in July,
wherever Silhouette books are sold.**

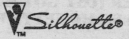